MY LORD WINTER

CAROLA DUNN

D0650694

Harlequin Books

TORONTO • NEW YORK • LONDON
AMSTERDAM • PARIS • SYDNEY • HAMBURG
STOCKHOLM • ATHENS • TOKYO • MILAN
MADRID • WARSAW • BUDAPEST • AUCKLAND

Published November 1992

ISBN 0-373-31186-9

MY LORD WINTER

CHAPTER ONE

EVEN AT Tom Coachman's cautious pace, the ancient travelling carriage, with its huge wheels and worn, old-fashioned springs, jolted horridly over the frozen ruts in the road. Miss Gracechurch breathed a sigh of relief as the spires of Oxford rose around them in the winter dusk.

Jane pulled her hand from her feather-filled muff, reached across the threadbare, once-green velvet seat and patted her governess's arm. "You can soon rest your aged bones, Gracie dear."

"Heavens, you make me sound as if I am approaching the grave. At six-and-thirty, I am younger than this dreadful vehicle."

"Yes, and see how far it has brought us, despite your misgivings. Two hundred miles from Hornby and only sixty to go to London."

"Wi' this hard frost, 'tain't like to rain, neither, my lady," put in the young abigail, Ella, hugging her cloak of grey duffle about her. "Pa said he can't promise the roof won't leak."

"Old Tom has done wonders to get it moving at all," said Jane, laughing.

As they turned into the yard of the Golden Cross, a wheel caught on some obstruction, then jerked free. The carriage continued for a few feet and drew to a halt before, like a rheumatic dog, it groaned and sank slowly and awkwardly onto its haunches.

"Mercy me!" squawked Ella, dropping her tatting to grab the strap. It broke off in her hand and she landed in Miss Gracechurch's lap. The bandboxes that had shared the seat with her tumbled to the floor.

Young Thomas appeared at the window, the smartness of his new maroon livery marred by the green and white muffler Jane had insisted he wear. He wrenched open the door. The lower hinge gave way and it sagged drunkenly.

"My lady!" he cried, "Ye're not hurt? Oh, lor'!" He seized his flustered sister round the waist and hoisted her out in a flurry of red flannel petticoats. Her round, pink cheeks took on a cherry hue in the icy air.

Miss Gracechurch straightened her bonnet, her smooth oval face no whit discomposed. "Well, my dear," she said to Jane, "I fear you were a trifle over-optimistic."

"Just a trifle," agreed Jane wryly as a splintering sound announced the demise of a wheel. The carriage tilted to the side. "Perhaps we had best extract ourselves before the roof comes down."

The stress of its new configuration had already parted one corner of the roof from the wall panels. Through the gap, a star winked down from the dusk-blue sky. Jane chose to regard it as a good omen.

Thomas leaned in and removed the bandboxes from around Miss Gracechurch's feet. He let down the steps, but their angle made them useless. To yells of encouragement from the crowd of ostlers, waiters, and passers-by, he lifted down first the governess and then his mistress. Jane had scarcely set foot on the cobbles when the glass in the far window shattered, spraying the interior with shards.

Old Tom stood there shaking his head, his weathered face gloomy above the green and white muffler matching his son's. "I warned 'e, m'lady. I warned 'e. T'rear axle jus' fell to pieces, jus' like that."

"How very fortunate," said Jane, "that it did not choose to do so miles from anywhere."

By then the landlord had appeared to send his servants scurrying about their business. He was less inclined to think it fortunate that the carriage had chosen the yard of the Golden Cross to expire in. "Irate" would more nearly have described his sentiments, but Miss Gracechurch took charge with her usual quiet competence.

"Lady Jane's coachman and footman will see to the proper disposal of the remains," she assured him in her light, clear voice. "In the meantime, we require a private parlour, a bedchamber for two, and accommodations for the two menservants and her ladyship's abigail. We shall dine at seven."

The scowl vanished from the innkeeper's face. Bowing, he ushered them into the inn and a few minutes later they were taking off their bonnets before a cheerful fire in a comfortable chamber.

"You were splendid, Gracie dear," said Jane, setting her bonnet carefully on the dressing table. Of royal blue velvet with a matching ostrich plume, it had been fashioned by the only milliner in Lancaster, after a design from *La Belle Assemblée*. It was quite the smartest she had ever owned. "After we scattered debris all over the premises on our arrival," she went on, "I expected a rough-and-tumble before the innkeeper would allow us to stay here."

"I beg you will not copy your brother's speech, Jane. Your mama will turn me off without a reference if she hears boxing cant issuing from your lips. As for mine host, the judicious mention of a title of nobility frequently clears the way of such difficulties, as I have told you before."

"It is sadly lowering—is it not?—that he did not relent for the sake of our pretty faces and charming smiles, but only because Papa is the Marquis of Hornby."

Miss Gracechurch laughed, her brown eyes lighting with amusement. Jane wished her own eyes were brown, not a commonplace, insipid blue. Their hair was amazingly similar in colour, a sadly dull, dark blond shade, but whereas the governess was forever trying to banish the delightful wisps and curls that escaped her severe coiffure, Jane's tresses refused to be coaxed into such frivolity. Straight they were, and straight, for all Ella could do, they would remain.

At least, after years of worry, Jane had at the age of eighteen attained the same height as Gracie. Though it was somewhat above average, she considered it the perfect height for an elegant female. Miss Gracechurch, even in her requisitely drab governess gowns, was the most elegant female of Jane's admittedly small acquaintance.

Except Mama, and she did not want to think about Mama.

"We shall have to hire a carriage to take us to London," she said, unfastening her blue velvet pelisse as the fire's warmth penetrated.

"My dear, I very much doubt I brought enough money with us for so great an expense. You may think it foolish of me, since our vehicle was known to be less than trustworthy, but I did not like to be responsible for a large sum while on the high road and staying at public inns.''

"Highwaymen, pickpockets, and thieving chambermaids, as in all the best novels?"

"They do exist, so do not laugh at me, you odious child. I wish I had succeeded in persuading you to wait for Lady Hornby to send her carriage to Lancashire. Now we shall have to apply to your parents for assistance anyway, as I had planned should we find ourselves in the briars."

"No! I *will* not wait meekly here until Mama finds a moment between parties, or Papa between Government meetings, to attend to our needs. She has already put me off twice with feeble excuses. I have missed two Seasons! At twenty, I am nearly at my last prayers."

"You have a year or two before you need consider yourself an ape-leader, my dear. Even elderly ladies of twenty are occasionally fortunate enough to find husbands."

"You may tease, Gracie, but I will not wait any longer. We shall take the stage coach."

"Impossible," said Miss Gracechurch, calm but firm. "The reverse of the many advantages of noble birth is that a course of action perfectly unexceptionable for a nobody is unacceptable for Lady Jane Brooke."

Jane had expected an outright rejection of the stage, which was why she had suggested it first. "The Mail, then," she next proposed. "That is more respectable than the stage, and faster, too, is it not?"

"Yes, but..."

"We need not mention my title. Jane Brooke is not an unusual name, so it will not draw attention, and no one in Society need know that I travelled by Mail. After all, the other passengers are scarce likely to turn up later at Almack's to confront me.''

"True. Nonetheless, I cannot like it.''

Sensing a weakening, Jane redoubled her efforts. Ella, when she brought in hot water for washing, added her mite in loyal support of her mistress. By the time they went down to dinner, Miss Gracechurch had capitulated.

Thomas, waiting in the parlour, was sent to put their names on the way-bill. "Reserve seats for three,'' Miss Gracechurch instructed him. "You and your father will have to follow later, with the trunks, after you have disposed of the sad remains.''

"And do not forget to say that I am *Miss* Brooke,'' Jane reminded him as he departed.

"Aye, *miss*.'' He grinned at her over his shoulder.

The parlour was small but cosy, with a table for two set in front of the fireplace. In need of exercise, Jane strolled about the room. She paused to examine a watercolour of Magdalen Bridge, but her mind was elsewhere.

"Ella shall pack away my new pelisse and bonnet,'' she decided. "They are too fine for plain Miss Jane Brooke who travels by the Mail. I do not wish to seem above my company.''

"Small danger of that,'' said Miss Gracechurch, warming her hands at the fire. "Indeed, I fear Lady Hornby will consider you by far too democratic in your notions.''

"When we reach St. James's Place I shall be properly high in the instep,'' she promised. "I shall never call you my dear Gracie, nor laugh and chatter with Ella. Mama shall see how well you have brought me up.''

"I hope so, my dear. If you will only remember to think before you speak!"

Thomas returned in time to serve dinner. He reported that the only places available on the morrow were two inside seats and one outside on the London-bound Manchester Mail, passing through Oxford at four in the afternoon.

"And arriving in London in the small hours of the morning," Miss Gracechurch groaned.

The next morning they spent walking about Oxford, having purchased a guide to the colleges. In the afternoon, carrying the small amount of baggage permitted, they arrived at the Mitre in good time and were ushered into the waiting room. Jane was enveloped in the cinnamon-brown kerseymere cloak and hood that had been her best before the purchase of the blue velvet pelisse. Though of excellent quality, for her father never begrudged sufficient funds, the cloak was suitable for the country with little pretense to fashion.

Miss Gracechurch was her usual quietly elegant self, but Ella looked like an overstuffed doll. She had donned every petticoat she possessed and borrowed both her brother's and her father's green-striped mufflers to wrap about her head. Two youthful gentlemen taking a late luncheon at a table in one corner of the room burst into laughter when they saw her.

"Not to worry, sweetheart," cried the shorter of the pair, nudging the other. "We'll keep you warm."

Miss Gracechurch frowned at them. The other quickly said, "Don't mind Hancock, ma'am. He's a bit above himself just now but he's really quite harmless."

"No offense meant, miss," Mr. Hancock assured Ella, standing up to reveal a glimpse of a pink and blue waistcoat between the huge brass buttons on his blue

coat. He bowed politely to Jane and Miss Gracechurch
and went on with an irrepressible grin, "I wager you are
waiting for the Mail, as we are?"

"I say, old chap, not at all the thing to ask a lady when
you haven't even been introduced."

"You introduced me," said his friend. "Near as
makes no difference. I'll return the favour. Pray allow
me to present the Honourable Aloysius Reid, ma'am.
We have both been rusticated for the rest of term."

Mr. Reid jumped up and bowed. A tall, lanky, so-
berly dressed youth, he was horrified by his friend's lack
of discretion. Jane took pity on him.

"How do you do, Mr. Reid, Mr. Hancock. Yes, we
are taking the Mail to London. My name is Jane Brooke,
and I am travelling with Miss Gracechurch."

The gentlemen bowed again, and Miss Gracechurch
nodded stiffly before drawing Jane away. "My dear, it
is most improper to introduce yourself to strangers in
such a manner."

"Mr. Reid seemed so downcast, I could not snub him,
and after all they do not know who I am."

"I can only hope they never find out!"

"What did Mr. Hancock mean, that they have been
rusticated?"

"They must be undergraduates who were caught in
some doubtless disgraceful scrape, and they have been
suspended from their studies."

Jane decided regretfully that decorum forbade her to
enquire as to the nature of the scrape. Nonetheless, when
Mr. Reid ventured a tentative remark about the weather,
she responded in her usual friendly manner, casting a
half guilty, half laughing glance at her governess.

A waiter came to warn them that the Mail was due in
a few minutes. The young men put on their greatcoats,

Mr. Reid's with three capes, Mr. Hancock's with half a dozen that made him look as broad as he was tall. They all went outside, where a team of four powerful horses stood ready, snorting and tossing their heads. Jane heard in the distance the *tantara* of the post horn and moments later the Royal Mail thundered into view.

She had no time to admire the smart red, black and gold coach. Everything happened at once: ostlers rushed to change the team; two passengers hurried to descend from within, a third from the coachman's box-seat; bags and parcels were retrieved from the front boot, others tossed in their place; the guard exchanged his sack of mail for another, which he deposited in the hind boot beneath his seat; Messrs. Hancock and Reid boosted Ella up to the roof and followed her; without quite knowing how she got there, Jane found herself sitting beside Gracie in the coach, catching her breath.

The post horn sounded again and they were on their way. "Heavens!" Jane favoured their fellow travellers with a sunny smile. "Now I know what is meant by 'post-haste.'"

The gentleman seated diagonally opposite returned her smile and raised his glossy beaver politely. His dark hair was touched with grey at the temples, lending a distinguished air to a rather long face with intelligent eyes. Jane like the look of him at once.

"Post-haste!" said the stout, red-faced man beside him in a belligerent tone. "Fast enough, happen, but for convenience and efficiency there's nowt like a private carriage for them as has the brass. I keep my own carriage, like any gentleman, and think it no extravagance."

Jane found herself absolutely unable to resist asking, "Then why are you on the Mail, sir?"

Mr. Josiah Ramsbottom's carriage, it transpired, was being re-upholstered in long-wearing Northampton leather, at great cost. Mr. Ramsbottom was only too eager to provide details of that cost in pounds, shillings, and pence. Mr. Ramsbottom, a Manchester cotton merchant, was a self-made man and proud of it.

The other passenger was less forthcoming, but despite Gracie's unobtrusive protests Jane succeeded in discovering that he was a lawyer returning to London after visiting a client. Once the ice was broken, Mr. Selwyn readily entered into a conversation about Oxford, where he had attended Jesus College. Having walked about the town, Jane had many questions for him. She was pleased when Miss Gracechurch set aside her scruples and joined in.

Mr. Ramsbottom declared that he had no opinion of book-learning and fell mercifully silent but for the odd interjection on the well-known poverty of scholars.

Happily occupied, Jane was surprised when the coach stopped at Crowmarsh Gifford to change horses. She let down the window, leaned out, and called, "Ella, are you all right up there? You are not excessively chilled?"

"No, my...miss," Ella called back, "'cepting my nose. I'm squeezed in cosy atween the young gentlemen."

"Very cosy, miss, I assure you," came Mr. Hancock's jaunty voice.

"You get a nice view from up here, *miss*," said Ella. "Right pretty it is, with the river and that. There's little sort o' curls o' mist dancing on the river."

Jane wished she had paid more attention to the scenery, though it would have been difficult with the windows steamed up. Perhaps she could step out for a moment—but no, the guard sounded the *tantara* on his yard of tin and they were off again.

Mr. Ramsbottom at once engaged her in a discussion of different types of cotton goods, their qualities and especially their prices. He was surprisingly interesting, and the information would have been useful, she thought, had she really been plain Miss Brooke who travelled by the Mail. Miss Gracechurch and Mr. Selwyn were talking about the education of women. Jane would have liked to listen, but that would have meant snubbing poor, vulgar Mr. Ramsbottom.

Her attention divided, she was vaguely aware that the coach had slowed, moving nearer a walking pace that its usual headlong dash. She rubbed at the window but the condensation seemed to be on the outside now.

"What's up?" enquired Mr. Ramsbottom, wiping the window beside him with a large, red, white-spotted handkerchief. "We ain't going post-haste now."

At that moment the coach lurched. Ella screamed. Several male voices swore. Wood creaked, cracked, and snapped. The coach gently tilted to one side and came to rest with the window pressed against a leafless, spiky hawthorn hedge.

"Not again!" Jane groaned.

CHAPTER TWO

"WE PASSED THE GATES o' Wintringham Abbey a hundred yards back," the coachman informed the little group huddled in the dense fog beside the wreck of the Manchester Mail. "Leastways, it's my belief we did, for all I couldn't see 'em. I knows this road like the back o' my hand. We can't go there."

"Why not?" demanded Mr. Ramsbottom belligerently.

"'Tis the Earl o' Wintringham's place, him they calls My Lord Winter. Winter by name and winter by nature, by all accounts. There ain't a stiffer, starchier, top-loftier nob in the kingdom. Throw us out on our ears, he would."

"Surely not!" Jane was incredulous. "You said the nearest village is at least two miles, and it will soon grow dark. We are stranded. He cannot in good conscience refuse us assistance."

"That's what you thinks, missy. Earls can do what they bloody well likes and to the devil wi' the rest of us."

"I say, mind your language, my good man," Mr. Reid protested. "Ladies present, don't you know." He blushed as Jane flashed him a smile of thanks. "All the same, Miss Brooke, I've heard of Lord Wintringham and I wager he'd be on his high ropes if we invaded."

"Curst cold-hearted cove," Mr. Hancock confirmed in a voice of doom.

"Whatever the rest of you choose to do," Jane said resolutely, "I intend to seek shelter at Wintringham Abbey. If I can find the place," she added on a less certain note, peering into the fog. The hedge on the other side of the ditch where the coach had come to rest was almost invisible. The breeze had dropped and the air was decidedly chilly.

"I am willing to lead the way," Mr. Selwyn offered. "I suggest we link hands so that no one who wishes to go is left behind. Miss Gracechurch, will you be so good as to take my hand?"

Miss Gracechurch complied. Jane took her other hand, and reached for Ella's. The others stepped forward, murmuring agreement.

"Wait!" cried the coachman. "You young coves give us a hand tying the baggage on them hosses, and I'll come along too. Ain't got nothink to lose, arter all."

When they set off a few minutes later, in single file, Jane could scarcely see the coachman at the rear end of the line, leading his three horses—the guard had bravely ridden off on the fourth beast with his precious mail sacks. The sound of plodding hooves and jingling harness was muffled by the fog, and for some reason they found themselves speaking in hushed voices. Mr. Selwyn kept to the side of the road. Very soon he came to a bridge of great slabs of stone laid across the ditch. He led his band over, the horses hooves ringing hollowly, and halted before towering gates of wrought iron.

"Locked."

"There must be a lodge," Jane said, "but no doubt the gatekeeper would turn us away. See if there is a wicket gate to one side."

This proved to be the case. With considerable difficulty and much low-voiced profanity the horses were persuaded to squeeze through, their muzzles wrapped in cloths to stop them neighing in protest. Jane was breathless with suppressed laughter as they started up the drive. She was quite looking forward to crossing swords with the haughty Earl of Wintringham.

Guided by white posts linked by black-painted chains, they quickly covered the half mile to the house. Judging by the vast sweep of steps they came upon, Wintringham Abbey must have been an impressive mansion, but even the front door was invisible from the bottom. Mr. Selwyn came to a stop.

"Perhaps we should look for the servants' entrance," he said hesitantly.

"We might never find it." Jane dropped Gracie's and Ella's hands and started up the steps. She knew they would follow. The coachman's plaintive "Don't forget me!" told her the others were coming, too.

To one side of double doors of iron-banded oak hung a brass bell-pull. She tugged on it twice and heard a clangour within, faint through the thick wood. As it died away, she moved to the centre of her little troop, facing the doors. The right-hand one swung open and she stepped in.

"Who... What...?"

Jane ignored the stammering footman in favour of the butler, who was advancing across the marble floor of the spacious, lofty hall.

"The Mail coach came to grief in the fog," she announced, pushing back her hood. "I and my companions have come to request shelter."

"Impossible, madam." Not an eyebrow twitched. "There is an inn in the next village."

"We cannot possibly go so far. I daresay this house is large enough to accommodate us without anyone even noticing."

"I fear her ladyship would disagree, madam. Peter will direct you to Nuffield." Indicating the footman, he turned away.

Young Mr. Hancock was not about to be cowed by a mere servant, however imposing. "You can't see your hand in front of your face out there," he said loudly.

Emboldened, Mr. Ramsbottom joined in with his customary belligerence. "What's more, it's demmed nearly dark."

"At least let the ladies stay," pleaded Mr. Reid.

A cold, quiet voice cut through the clamour. "Bradbury, who are these intruders?"

The butler swung round. "My lord!"

Jane looked with interest at the infamous earl. Her gaze met icy grey eyes set in a square-chinned face that would have been handsome but for its unrelenting hauteur. Lord Wintringham's hair was dark, cropped short above a broad brow. Tall and powerful, he wore a superbly tailored shooting jacket, buckskin breeches, and top-boots with an air of formality more suited to evening dress. The wrathful flare of his nostrils belied his apparent calm composure.

Jane had pictured an elderly curmudgeon. My Lord Winter was no more than thirty years of age.

Moving towards him, she curtsied. Now was the moment to solve all their problems with what Gracie had called a judicious mention of her title of nobility. Jane easily resisted the temptation. Even if so toplofty a gentleman were willing to believe a shabby young woman from the Mail coach to be a marquis's daughter, she was determined to best him on her own terms.

"Lord Wintringham?" She favoured him with a sunny smile, unaware that imps of mischief danced in her eyes. "I am Jane Brooke. I beg your pardon for this invasion, but we are in dire need of a refuge. The Mail coach overturned."

He looked her up and down and his lips curled in contempt. "I daresay Bradbury can direct you to the nearest inn, madam."

"I daresay you have not glanced through a window recently, my lord," she retorted. "The fog is so impenetrable we were hard put to find your vast mansion."

"Hardly impenetrable, Miss Brooke, since you have penetrated it." He raised supercilious eyebrows at his butler.

"The mist does seem to have thickened, my lord," admitted that individual with evident reluctance.

Jane returned to the attack. "Miss Gracechurch, the lady with whom I am travelling, cannot go a step farther." From the corner of her eye she saw Gracie suddenly lean heavily on Mr. Selwyn's arm with a failing expression. "And her maid has a shocking cold."

For a moment she was afraid she had done it too brown as Ella's prompt sneeze emerged, intermixed with a giggle. However, the earl, uninterested in a mere maidservant, was regarding Miss Gracechurch with a slight frown.

"Forgive me, ma'am," he said to her abruptly. "I have no desire to figure as an inhospitable misanthrope. Bradbury will see to your comfort." He turned away.

The butler stared after his master in dismay, his mouth opening and closing as if he wished to ask for elucidation but didn't quite dare. Jane bit her lip. The poor man must be wondering whether Gracie was to be offered a chair or a bedchamber, not to mention what he was to do with the rest of the uninvited visitors.

Jane was perfectly prepared to assume command, but before his lordship had taken more than two strides he was stopped by an imperious voice.

"Wintringham!" The elderly lady's gown of grey figured silk, lavishly embellished with Valenciennes to match her lace cap, suggested widowhood. Despite the formal way she addressed his lordship, Jane guessed she must be the dowager countess, though they had no features in common but the coldness of their gaze. "Wintringham, who are these..." she raised a lorgnette and studied the interlopers with austere disapprobation "...these persons?"

"Stranded travellers, ma'am. The fog is become impassable. I feel compelled to offer the hospitality of the Abbey."

"Indeed! And am I to have no say in my own house?"

"Naturally, ma'am, you will wish to instruct Bradbury as to which accommodations are to be prepared for our...guests."

Short of arguing with his lordship before their inferiors, the countess had little choice but to comply. Neatly manœuvred! Jane nearly applauded. She caught Mr. Selwyn's eye and saw that he found the situation decidedly entertaining. He patted Gracie's hand. Gracie was struggling with mixed emotions, caught between amusement and trepidation.

Curtsying to Lady Wintringham, Jane said, "We are in sore straits, my lady. It is excessively kind of you to take us in. As you see, we are seven passengers, and the unfortunate coachman is waiting outside with our bags and three horses."

"Allow me to present Miss Jane Brooke, ma'am,"
said the earl. "Miss Brooke appears to be the appointed
spokeswoman."

Was that a glint of mockery in his eyes, or merely irritation? Before Jane could make up her mind, he excused himself, bowed, and strode away.

Edmund Neville, Earl of Wintringham, was aware
only of irritation. He retired to his library to brood over
the invasion of his home led by an impudent young
woman whose blue eyes had seemed to laugh at him.
He'd have been inclined to throw them all out to fend for
themselves but for the opportunity they offered to
thwart her ladyship for once. Nothing would persuade
the dowager to brangle with him in public.

Also, he had felt sorry for the older female—Chur-
chill? No, Gracechurch. She was obviously exhausted
and she looked respectable, probably a gentlewoman
come down in the world. The rest he dismissed as a
horde of Cits.

Not that anything could be worse than the house party
presently assembled at the Abbey, he thought bitterly.
He had invited Fitz for a little light relief, and Fitz had
turned up with his very pregnant wife, who ought to be
decently secluded at home, and her sister. The reason
was all too plain to Edmund: the Honourable Lavinia
Chatterton was setting her cap at him.

The worst of it was that Lady Wintringham had taken
it into her head to support the chit. Lavinia was of noble birth, well-dowered, pretty enough in a childish way,
and possessed of all the social graces. The countess had
decided that it was time for her nephew to marry and she
would harass him unmercifully until he complied.

Edmund poured himself a glass of Madeira and
slumped with a groan into one of the deep leather chairs

by the fireplace. For once the mere contemplation of his library brought no solace. Two stories high, with a gallery half way up, it was a handsome room large enough for a long table, a desk, and several comfortable chairs. Bookshelves reached from floor to ceiling, interrupted only by two tall windows at one end. A servant had already closed the crimson velvet curtains, shutting out the night and the accursed fog.

Sipping his wine, Edmund stared into the glowing coals in the grate. A fire always burned here in cold or damp weather, both to preserve the books and because this was his sanctuary, inherited from his uncle along with title, vast estates, and vaster responsibilities. On the infrequent occasions when he thought of his uncle, he pictured him poring over a medieval Herbal or a first edition of Chapman.

Whenever Edmund acquired a rare volume, he wished he had known the late earl better and could share with him his pleasure in expanding the superb collection. Now, however, all he wanted was something to distract him for half an hour. A traveller's tale, perhaps...

The door opened. "You there, Ned?" enquired a cheerful voice. "Ah yes, there you are. I thought you'd have gone to earth in here among your precious books. What a hullaballoo!"

"Do come in, Fitz," said Edmund ironically as his friend helped himself to Madeira and dropped into the opposite chair.

Not a whit disconcerted, Lord Fitzgerald raised his glass in salute. "Cheers. Her ladyship's in high fidgets, I hear."

"Come now, have you ever seen my aunt in high fidgets?"

"Well, no, but Miss Neville says she's cross as a bear at a stake."

"I might have known my cousin Neville would spread word of the deplorable influx."

"I must say, I'd have thought you'd be glad of any additions to the company. Not that I'm complaining, mind you," Fitz hastened to add. "Devilish good of you to put up with Lavinia and my poor Daphne."

"Lady Fitzgerald must always be a welcome guest," said Edmund with more politeness than truth, for he found the lady insipid. He did not go so far as to pronounce Lavinia welcome. "However, the new arrivals can scarcely be counted as assets to our company. I suppose they will dine in the servants' hall, or in the housekeeper's room."

"Passengers on the Mail, weren't they? Took the Mail myself once or twice, in my misspent youth."

"You prove my point." My Lord Winter grinned, a sight few had ever been privileged to witness. The grin was wiped from his face as the library door opened again.

"Fitz? Daphne asked me to tell you... Oh, my lord!" As the gentlemen rose to their feet, Lavinia abandoned her pretense of conveying a message from her sister. "I was prodigious shocked to hear of those dreadful people pushing their way into the Abbey. You are excessively charitable, I vow, to permit them to stay."

"I had little choice, Miss Chatterton. The fog is... er... impenetrable."

"Still, I think you are prodigious kind. Miss Neville said one of them is a disgracefully impertinent girl, a despicable creature."

"Miss Brooke was certainly outspoken." Perversely, Edmund found himself coming to the young woman's defence. "She was concerned for a fellow-traveller, I believe, who was in some distress."

"A ploy to gain your sympathy, no doubt," Lavinia sniffed. "Such vulgar people are beneath one's notice."

"I daresay you will wish to take dinner on a tray in your chamber, then, Miss Chatterton. Certain of my unexpected guests will be dining with us." He ignored Fitz's raised eyebrows.

"You are hoaxing me, sir!"

"On the contrary, ma'am," he said coldly. "I am not accustomed to hoax."

Her eyes widened in alarm. "Of course, my lord, if you think it proper..." she gabbled. "Pray do not suppose that I mistrust your judgement.... Excuse me; I must go and see if Daphne needs me."

"What was it Daphne sent you to tell me?" enquired her brother-in-law.

"To tell you? Oh, nothing important, Fitz. I have forgotten it. You had best ask her yourself. You cannot expect me to recall every trifling whim." Miss Chatterton flounced from the room.

"Little minx," said Lord Fitzgerald. "A transparent excuse, if ever I heard one. I'm sorry, Ned, I'll have a word with her about pursuing you in here. I shouldn't have brought her, but my mama-in-law, you know..."

"Few could withstand the combined forces of Lady Chatterton and my aunt."

"*You* could, I wager, and can, and will. Tell me about this Miss Brooke of yours. A beauty, is she?"

"No, passable but nothing beyond the ordinary." Edmund remembered mocking blue eyes. "A saucy wench. And she is not *my* Miss Brooke."

"I suppose she is fit to sit down at table with gently bred females?" Fitz asked. "You said at first they were to dine in the servants' hall."

"What, you don't trust my judgement? She was, as I said, outspoken, but not vulgar. Miss Gracechurch, the older woman, had something of refinement in her air, I fancy." He reached for the bell-pull and rang. "I shall leave it to Bradbury to sort the sheep from the goats."

A footman appeared on the instant and was sent for the butler. Bradbury received his instructions in stolid silence, but Edmund recognized his deep disapproval. Was the servant yet higher in the instep than his master? No, for already Lord Wintringham regretted the impulse that had made him lower his standards for the sake of giving Lavinia a set-down.

Bradbury bowed and departed.

"So you really mean to go through with it," marvelled Fitz. "Of all men, you're the least likely..."

"Enough of my unbidden guests," Edmund said impatiently. "Will you play backgammon?"

"Make it billiards and you're on."

Since Lord Fitzgerald regarded backgammon as an intellectual pursuit and had an oft-expressed aversion to all things intellectual, Edmund acquiesced. He left his sanctuary with considerable reluctance, praying that neither his whining brother-in-law nor his hearty cousin-in-law would be found in the billiard room.

Thus far he was in luck, but there his luck deserted him. After three games, Fitz went up to change for dinner fifteen guineas the richer.

Edmund repaired to his apartment. His valet, Alfred, awaited him in the dressing-room with hot water, freshly pressed evening clothes, and unabashed curiosity.

"Your lordship's set the hen-house in a right flutter," he observed, shaking out his master's jacket.

"You are referring to a certain consternation in the servants' quarters, I take it."

"That I am. There's them as can't think what's got into your lordship to invite them Mail coach people to sit down at table with you. Your razor, my lord."

"Thank you." Edmund smoothed his chin with the straight-edged blade, speaking out of the corner of his mouth. "It was a momentary whim, Alfred, to put Miss Chatterton in her place for considering them beneath her touch. It's devilish difficult to find an excuse to snub Miss Chatterton when her sister is married to my friend, especially as her ladyship favours the girl."

"So that's the way of it." The servant nodded wisely. "I reckoned summat of the sort."

"You will not speak of it, however!"

"'Course not, my lord," said Alfred, injured. "I don't never gossip about our affairs."

"I know it, man, though I cannot think why not, since you are an incorrigible gossipmonger." Edmund washed the soap off his face and reached for the ready-warmed towel. "Tell me with whom I shall be dining tonight."

"Well now, there's Mr. Selwyn. A lawyer, he is, and a pleasant-spoken gentleman by all accounts. Then there's a couple of young sprigs, Mr. Hancock and the Honourable Mr. Reid. Mr. Bradbury suspicions they've been sent down from the university. But the one what's exercising Mr. Bradbury's mind, as you might say, is a fella by name of Ramsbottom. Mr. Josiah Ramsbottom. Your shirt, my lord."

"Ramsbottom?" Donning the snow-white, ruffled shirt, Edmund grimaced, wishing again that he had sternly repressed his whim, as was his custom.

"Collar too tight, my lord?"

"No, no. What's wrong with this Ramsbottom?"

"Downright vulgar, not to mince words. But he won't take no for an answer. Claims he was an inside passenger and if them young chaps as rode outside gets to dine with the nobs, he's entitled."

"Entitled!"

"Says he could buy up the rest of 'em ten times over and it's honest merchants as makes this country great."

Turning to the mirror to tie his neckcloth, Edmund caught his valet's knowing eye and grinned. "It sounds as if Mr. Ramsbottom will enliven the conversation no end. Am I to entertain the coachman, also?"

"Lord, no! Nor the abigail, neither. She's a likely lass, that one."

"And her mistress?"

"Miss Gracechurch? She's a lady, sure enough. Even Mr. Bradbury says so. Gentry fallen on hard times. Off to visit relatives, like as not."

"There is a third female, is there not?"

"Miss Brooke. A bold hussy, Mr. Bradbury says. Going to Town to try for a governess or companion, most like, but she won't get no respectable position if she don't mend her ways—Mr. Bradbury says."

Edmund gritted his teeth and tossed the ruined neckcloth on the floor, reaching for another. He suspected Alfred was teasing him but he could not tax him with it without confessing to an unwarranted interest in Miss Brooke. "And does Mr. Bradbury say whether this 'bold hussy' is to 'dine with the nobs'?" he asked casually.

Alfred looked up at the ceiling for inspiration. "Let me see, now, what did he say? Ah, I have it. Being as how your lordship interduced Miss Brooke to her ladyship, he don't feel like he has no choice in the matter. But he ain't happy, my lord, he ain't happy."

Another neckcloth landed on the floor. "Believe me," said My Lord Winter dryly, "nor am I."

CHAPTER THREE

JANE GAZED IN DISMAY at her new blue merino travelling dress. "Why did the wretched man go and ask us to dine with himself and Lady Wintringham?" she moaned. "He must have guessed I don't have an evening gown with me."

Commiserating, Ella shook her head. "It's a good job we kept your best by us so's you'd be respectable arriving in St. James's Place. Just think, it could be packed away in your trunk, back in Oxford."

"I suppose so. It will have to do. After all, it scarcely matters since My Lord Winter and her ladyship already hold me in disdain."

"There's more than just them, my lady—Miss Jane, I should say. Quite a party, the housekeeper says."

"Does that man wish to humiliate me before his friends?" Jane demanded indignantly, just as Miss Gracechurch came into the comfortable, though small and plainly furnished, chamber.

"If it is the earl you are referring to, Jane, he may be haughty, but I hesitate to believe him malicious."

"Only because it was when I said your strength was failing that he relented and let us stay."

"Oh dear, I cannot think what came over me, to aid and abet your tarradiddles! If the marchioness ever hears of it, she will turn me away not only without a reference but without a character."

"I shall say that you strenuously opposed my wilful behaviour. But Mama will never hear of it."

"I wish I could be so sanguine. As long as it was only the coach passengers who knew you as Miss Brooke, there was little danger, but you will be moving in the same circles as the Wintringhams in London."

"Perhaps they will not go to London. Ella, see if you can find out from the housekeeper."

"Shouldn't think so, miss. She's near as high-and-mighty as the countess. But his lordship's gentleman's a friendly chap. I'll try him."

"Do. Of course, that still leaves all their guests to be met with in Town. I wish the wretched man had not invited us to dine with them. My first ever formal dinner is like to prove a disaster! Is it too late to refuse?"

"Too late, and the height of rudeness when his lordship has been so condescending," said Miss Gracechurch firmly. "Hurry up and dress, Jane, or we shall be the last down."

"There's miles of corridors," said Ella, slipping the despised blue gown over Jane's head. "I'd best ring for a servant to show the way or you might get lost and miss your dinners."

"That would never do. Luncheon in Oxford seems an age ago and we landed in the ditch just about teatime. But don't worry, Gracie, I shall not put you to the blush by displaying an unladylike appetite."

"My dear, since no one knows I am your governess, if you gobble your food you will put none but yourself to the blush."

"True." Jane laughed, then studied her face in the mirror as Ella tidied her hair. With the severe style dictated by its straightness, she looked more like a governess than Gracie did. Oh, for a curl or two!

A chambermaid led them through passages, round corners, up and down steps, to the top of the grand staircase descending to the great hall. As she laid her hand on the baluster rail, Jane became aware of another deficiency in her dress. No gloves. Gracie had taught her that gloves must be worn to a formal dinner, yet she could scarcely have appeared in the drawing-room in her fur-lined mittens.

A glance told her that her mentor's hands were equally bare. Ah, well, there was no sense in repining. Her head held high, she started down the stairs with all the grace and dignity she could muster.

Her audience consisted of two ramrod-stiff footmen in grey livery piped with scarlet, and the supercilious butler. The latter stepped forward with a bow that was little more than a nod, nicely calculated to depress pretensions without being outright insolent.

"This way, if you please."

Taking her cue from Miss Gracechurch, Jane followed him without deigning to answer, her pretensions undepressed. The dozen pairs of eyes that turned to stare as Bradbury ushered them into the drawing room were more daunting.

"Miss Gracechurch, Miss Brooke," he said woodenly, and departed.

For a moment no one moved. Jane wondered whether she ought to curtsy, then decided she had rather be thought presumptuous than meek. She looked with interest at the assembled company.

Lord Wintringham stood near the fireplace, magnificent in evening dress but wearing an expression of insufferable arrogance. A short, thin gentleman of about the same age lounged beside him, leaning against the mantel in a much more relaxed attitude and consider-

ably more dandified apparel. The third in the group was
a fair young lady whose pretty face revealed both contempt and animosity. Her gown of pale rose sarcenet
trimmed with ribbons and rouleaux filled Jane with
envy.

Her gaze moved on. Slightly apart from the three, a
second young lady perched awkwardly on a straight
chair. She was obviously pregnant, very pregnant if Jane
was any judge—no, not pregnant, *in the family way* was
the polite phrase. Whatever one called it, to be present
in that condition she must surely live here, though Ella
had discovered the earl was unmarried. Her head was
turned towards the door, yet she had no interest in the
newcomers. She had a remote, inward look that Jane
recognized.

Two matrons in their thirties or early forties, ele-
gantly dressed and bejewelled, sat on a gold velvet love
seat. The older bore a startling resemblance to the dowager countess, right down to the cold, censorious expression of pride. The other appeared more discontented
than proud. Behind the loveseat stood two gentlemen
whom Jane guessed to be their husbands, a red-faced
squire and a weak-chinned nonentity.

On the other side of the fireplace Lady Wintringham
surveyed her unwelcome guests through her lorgnette,
her back ramrod straight. An elderly lady in black sat
next to her, with a white-haired gentleman on a chair
beside them. A small, plump woman in lavender hov-
ered nearby.

It seemed to Jane that an age had passed since the
butler had announced her and Gracie, but she supposed
it could not be more than a few seconds. Was no one
going to introduce them? With relief, she saw Mr. Selwyn and the two disgraced students, standing to one side

in an uncomfortable group. She smiled at them and noted equal relief in their answering smiles.

Heartened, Jane looked at Lord Wintringham again. The awkward pause lengthened. The young man leaning against the mantel stirred uneasily and Lord Wintringham glanced at the dowager, who made no move to carry out her duties as hostess. He came over to them.

"Allow me to make you known to everyone," he said stiffly. "You have met my aunt, Lady Wintringham, I believe."

Jane curtsied, Miss Gracechurch gave a slight bow, and the earl went on to introduce the elderly couple and the plump lady, "My cousin, Miss Neville." As he moved on around the room, presenting them to friends and relatives, Jane was sure she'd never remember all the names, let alone whom they belonged to. However, as they came to the contemptuous young lady, the drawing-room door swung open and Mr. Josiah Ramsbottom made a grand entrance.

"Evenin', all." His natural belligerence was diluted with genial self-satisfaction. Absorbing the impact of his brown-and-blue checked coat, his cherry-red waistcoat, and his daffodil-yellow knee-breeches, Jane at once felt her travelling dress to be quite acceptable. "Ye've a fine place here, my lord, my lady," Mr. Ramsbottom continued. "Must cost a mint o' brass to keep it up. Ye'd do better, happen, to tear the old parts down."

In the stunned silence that greeted this advice, Bradbury's announcement of dinner brought a visible relaxation. The bustle that accompanied the removal to the dining room permitted Mr. Ramsbottom's shocking effrontery to be discreetly ignored.

The Honourable Miss Chatterton stepped forward as if to claim Lord Wintringham's escort. The earl at once turned to Jane, standing beside him, and offered his arm. Surprised, she smiled at him and laid her hand on his arm, only to be reminded of her glovelessness. He did not appear to notice, but nor did he return her smile or show any sign of gratification at having her for his dinner partner. His face might have been carved in marble.

Miss Chatterton, on the other hand, scowled resentfully at Jane and whispered loudly to her sister, Lady Fitzgerald, "Look, Daphne, they have no gloves! What a pair of provincial dowds."

"Hush, Lavinia," said Lady Fitzgerald as her solicitous husband helped her to stand up.

"Stands to reason they didn't expect to need evening dress, travelling on the Mail," pointed out Lord Fitzgerald.

Jane was pleased to find him seated beside her at the dinner table. However, the rules Miss Gracechurch had taught her dictated that she devote her attention to her partner during the first course.

She took a sip of the consommé, served in exquisite Meissen porcelain, and said to the earl, "This soup is delicious, my lord. Have you a French cook?"

"No," he grunted.

"German china!" rang out Mr. Ramsbottom's voice from farther down the table. "To my mind, there's nowt to beat Worcester, or Crown Derby. Support British manufactories, that's my motto. Not that I'd waste the ready on fine china for the servants to be breaking with their clumsiness."

Inevitably, an unfortunate footman promptly dropped a soup plate, and Bradbury, with no more than a twitch of one fingertip, sent him from the room in disgrace. After a startled pause, the subdued murmur of conversation resumed.

Jane tried again. "Hot soup is particularly welcome in such cold weather as we have been having. In the north, the frosts have been unusually severe this year. Has it been the same in the south, my lord?"

"No."

"Not for me, me lad." Mr. Ramsbottom waved away a footman. "Consommy you can call it but it looks to me like the stuff we give 'em in the poorhouse in Manchester. Fills the belly but it don't put flesh on a man's bones. Give me good roast beef any day, and I will say a spot o' Yorkshire pudding goes down nice, for all I'm a Lancashire man." His remarks were addressed to the whole table, but little Miss Neville cowered, scarlet-faced, at his side as if she were to blame. Everyone else pretended they didn't hear.

Jane persevered with her own difficult neighbour. "I was unable to see the countryside for the fog. I daresay it is very pretty, with the Thames flowing nearby?"

"Pretty enough."

Two consecutive words! Congratulating herself, she pressed on. "Does the river cross your land, my lord?"

"It forms one boundary."

"Fish!" The word exploded from Mr. Ramsbottom's lips as the soup was removed with a large turbot in lobster sauce, a dish of eels, and various vegetables. "You might as well throw good money into the sea as waste it on having fish carried up from the coast when you live so far inland, and there's always good river fish to be had. Not but what turbot's a fine dish, but extravagance is what I don't hold with. I'll take some o' those eels, too, young feller-me-lad."

"Do you fish in the Thames, my lord?" Jane asked quickly.

"Occasionally."

"Have you rowboats, or punts?"

"No."

"The river bank must be a delightful place to hold picnics?"

The earl vouchsafed no answer, presumably unable to find one short enough. Jane gave up and concentrated on her dinner. She couldn't help wondering why My Lord Winter had chosen to seat her at his side if he had no desire to converse with her.

"Ah, here comes the solid victuals," observed Mr. Ramsbottom with satisfaction as the second course arrived—a baron of beef, a leg of mutton, and various ragoûts and fricassees. "I don't hold wi' them fancy sauces, though. Often as not they're just a way to hide second-rate meat, and the cook's pocketed the difference. Not that I'm saying your ladyship would let 'em get away with it!" He bowed gallantly to Lady Wintringham, beaming.

Her ladyship failed to appreciate the compliment. Her glare would have frozen a lesser man to the core, but Josiah Ramsbottom applied himself to his "solid victuals" with undiminished cheer. For some time no more was heard from him but an occasional demand for another slice of beef.

Jane turned to Lord Fitzgerald. He grinned at her and remarked, "Interesting chap, that. Did you travel far with him?"

"Only from Oxford, thank heaven. Mr. Ramsbottom gave me a great deal of useful information on how to avoid being cheated when buying muslins."

"I must get him to tell me how to avoid being cheated by my tailor!" He embarked on a long and involved story about an argument with Weston over a set of gilt buttons, interrupted now and then by his rather asinine laugh. Jane failed to grasp the point of the story, except that the tailor had won, but she didn't mind. At least Lord Fitzgerald was friendly and good-natured. She liked the way he turned frequently to his wife, on his other side, urging her to eat a morsel to keep up her strength.

Though Jane would have liked to discuss Lady Fitzgerald's pregnancy with his lordship, she knew the subject was considered indelicate. Once or twice she caught Gracie glancing at her anxiously and would have liked to reassure her that she was minding her tongue. Then she realized that Gracie was actually concerned about Lady Fitzgerald. The urge to speak out redoubled, but Jane restrained herself.

Gracie was sitting beside Mr. Selwyn. Jane had noticed them talking together during the first course. Now Gracie was attempting to converse with the lacklustre gentleman to whom they had not been introduced owing to Mr. Ramsbottom's eruption into the drawing-room. The gentleman appeared to be as monosyllabic as Lord Wintringham.

The earl was now well matched. His other neighbour was the lady who so closely resembled his aunt, and she made no effort to break his silence.

Jane laughed at the conclusion of Lord Fitzgerald's story and asked him a question which started him off on another. A remove of game pies and roast fowl came and went, and was succeeded by a third course of fruit pies, pastries, jellies, cheeses, and savouries. Mr. Ramsbottom pronounced his contempt for such *fal-lals*. Jane turned back to Lord Wintringham.

He looked unutterably bored. She resolved to break his reserve or die trying.

CHAPTER FOUR

WITH MINGLED DISMAY and curiosity, Edmund observed the glint of determination in Miss Brooke's blue eyes. What notion had the chit taken into her head now? So far, she had behaved with surprising propriety, even laughing at Fitz's dullest stories.

However captivating her laugh, Edmund had no intention of attempting to amuse her. She was useful as a foil against Lavinia, but he owed her no especial courtesy. On the contrary, in fact. He feared that by bringing her in to dinner he had set her up in her own conceit and he might be forced to give her a set-down.

Nonetheless, he awaited her words with no little interest. Anything must be preferable to his cousin Amelia's disdainful silence.

"I must beg a favour, my lord," Miss Brooke began, and he automatically stiffened in preparation for refusing whatever encroaching petition she uttered. "Would you mind telling me who everyone is? You see, I have been little in company and I have not the knack of remembering names. Besides, you were interrupted when you were so kindly introducing us to your guests."

"If you wish." He felt a ridiculous sense of disappointment at so ordinary a request. "Next to me is my cousin, Lady Amelia Danforth. She is Lady Wintringham's daughter."

"I guessed as much. They are very alike, are they not?" Miss Brooke had the wit to speak softly—and the effrontery to raise her nose in the air and peer down it superciliously. She had caught Amelia's expression to the life, and Edmund could not prevent his lips twitching. What was worse, she saw it, damn her impudence.

"Lady Amelia and my aunt are both uncommonly fastidious," he said coldly. She was unabashed. "Next to my cousin is my brother-in-law, Mr. Henry Parmenter," he continued. Parmenter bore an undeniable resemblance to a codfish—a boiled codfish, at that. Miss Brooke wisely made no attempt at mimicry.

"Hmm," was all she said, but she gave him a commiserating look.

"Miss Gracechurch and Mr. Selwyn you know. Miss Neville is a distant cousin of mine who acts as companion to my aunt."

"She seems sadly woebegone."

Edmund had scarcely noticed his poor relation for a long time. Now he saw that she was indeed in low spirits, with lines of tiredness and anxiety on her plump, round face. The position of companion to Lady Wintringham was no sinecure. There had been some talk awhile since of Miss Neville's going to keep house for a widowed brother, but her ladyship had declared that she could not manage without her. Should he have taken the trouble to ensure that his little cousin followed her own inclination?

He resented Miss Brooke's disturbing his conscience. "No doubt you would be woebegone if obliged to sit beside the Manchester merchant," he snapped.

"Not at all. Mr. Ramsbottom's manners leave something to be desired, admittedly, but he is not by any means difficult to converse with."

Her quizzical expression brought a tide of heat to his cheeks. He had not been put to the blush in years and it did nothing to improve his temper. He had no desire to continue the conversation, but if he fell silent now, he would be proving her point.

"My sister, Mrs. Parmenter, is next." Wife of the codfish. He dared her to comment. "Then the Honourable Eustace Tuttle. He and his wife are old friends of my aunt." Toad-eaters who bolstered her high opinion of herself and were often to be found living in clover at the Abbey, hanging upon his sleeve—to mix several metaphors. "Lady Wintringham you recall, I trust. Then one of the two young men you brought with you, I forget his name."

"I cannot see from here without peering. Tall and apologetic or short and chirpy?"

Again his lips twitched involuntarily. "Tall and apologetic, ma'am."

"The Honourable Aloysius Reid. You see, we had aristocratic company on the Mail, though Mr. Reid rode outside so I had no opportunity to become better acquainted."

"I see." He wondered if she was on the catch for a noble husband to save her from the miserable life of a governess. So bold a female would have little trouble entrapping a meek youth like Reid. Edmund disliked the thought intensely. He would keep an eye on the two while they were under his roof, he promised himself.

"And beside Mr. Reid?" she queried.

"Mrs. Tuttle, my aunt's friend, and beside her, Lady Amelia's husband, Lord Danforth." A good enough fellow if one expected no more of a man than to keep his acres in order, ride bruisingly to hounds, and drink himself into a stupor after dinner. Still, Cousin Amelia seemed satisfied to lord it over her rural neighbours.

"The gentleman who looks like a country squ . . . as if he enjoys country pursuits?"

Miss Brooke had a devilish penetrating eye to go with her unbridled tongue! "The Danforths spend most of their time in the country," he admitted grudgingly.

"Do you often go up to Town, my lord?" she asked. Though the question was casual, he gained the impression that she was more than a trifle anxious about his answer.

"I do not care for the Season's entertainments. I go up occasionally to speak in the House of Lords and to attend the theatre and the opera." And for auctions of rare books, but a provincial miss would scarcely be interested in those.

Rather than pepper him with questions about the theatre and the opera, Miss Brooke returned with an unexpected air of relief to the subject of his present guests. "Since Lord Fitzgerald is beside me, and his lady beside him, Miss Chatterton and Mr. Hancock must be in between?"

"Yes, and they are flirting abominably." The moment the words passed his lips, Edmund wished them unsaid. He was descending to her level and Lavinia's coquetry was none of her business. Nor did he consider it his business. If the girl hoped to make him jealous she was going to catch cold.

Miss Brooke giggled. "I cannot say I am surprised. I believe Mr. Hancock to be a confirmed flirt."

"Indeed," he said with quelling hauteur.

"I beg your pardon, I should not make light of it, only I did not suppose you enamoured of Miss Chatterton?"

Ignoring her enquiring tone, Edmund took refuge in silence.

Jane accepted his retreat philosophically. Not only had she succeeded far beyond her expectations in drawing him out, she had nearly made him smile, and she had discovered that he did not attend Society parties. He was something of a recluse, she suspected, not surprisingly since he refused to put himself to the trouble of making himself agreeable.

Of course, she was glad there was little risk of meeting My Lord Winter in London. Still, once or twice she had caught hints that beneath that icily handsome mask lurked a human being, and she rather regretted having no chance of coming to know him better. The fog was bound to clear in the night and tomorrow she and Gracie and Ella would resume their journey to Town.

In the meantime, she was soon going to have to face the ladies without the buffer provided by their menfolk. Thank heaven Gracie would be by her side.

She was just wondering whether she could possibly fit in one of the delicious-looking *mille-feuilles* on a nearby dish, when Lady Wintringham gave the signal to the ladies to withdraw. Jane and Miss Gracechurch followed the others to the drawing-room, walking behind the awkwardly moving Lady Fitzgerald, who leaned on her sister's arm.

Lady Wintringham sent Miss Neville to find her embroidery and, as soon as Lady Fitzgerald was settled on a chair, she summoned Miss Chatterton to her side. The elderly Mrs. Tuttle joined them by the fire. Lady Amelia crossed to a small escritoire and began to write. Mrs. Parmenter, with an unfriendly glance at Jane and Gracie, took a seat near Lady Fitzgerald and said something to her that made her utter a faint protest.

"I am worried about that young woman," Gracie murmured to Jane. "If I am not mistaken, she is near her time. Do you look out of the window, my dear, and see whether the fog has lifted yet."

Jane went across the long room to one of the tall windows, parted the heavy olive-green velvet curtains, and peered out. A pale blankness reflected her face and the yellow glow of candle and firelight.

"Miss Brooke!" said Lady Wintringham sharply. "Pray close the curtains at once."

"What can you be thinking of? We shall catch our deaths of cold," Mrs. Tuttle seconded her, adding in a slightly lower voice, "The lower classes have no notion how those of refined sensibilities suffer from the least draught."

Miss Chatterton shivered ostentatiously.

The Princess and the Pea, thought Jane, smothering a smile as she pulled the curtains together. She might have felt the chill herself had she been wearing thin silk instead of warm wool. The atmosphere was chilly enough, despite the blazing fire, and the stiffly elegant furnishings added no warmth of comfort.

Returning to Gracie, she overheard Lady Wintringham reproving Miss Chatterton for being too familiar with Mr. Hancock. "If you think to make Wintringham jealous," she said, "I can assure you that only a young lady of the most unexceptionable conduct has the slightest chance of winning his regard. My nephew is a highstickler. Regrettably your father is a mere baron, but I have made an exception in your case because..."

Regretfully, Jane moved out of earshot. No doubt Miss Chatterton had connexions of the highest rank, allowing her to aspire to the earl's hand. She wished them joy of each other.

Miss Gracechurch had seated herself at a small table with a chequered top of inlaid ivory and ebony. Jane took the second chair and reported that the fog was as thick as ever.

"Oh dear! Well, it cannot be helped. We must hope that Lady Fitzgerald has calculated her months correctly, since I cannot believe her husband would have brought her from home had she known she was due to give birth."

"No, he seems prodigious fond of her. Perhaps she is carrying twins."

"Perhaps. You found Lord Fitzgerald a congenial neighbour at dinner, did you not?"

"A bore, but a friendly bore."

"And our host? I fear he broke off your conversation abruptly, and with displeasure."

"It was a triumph to draw him into conversation at all. All my polite and unexceptionable openings he squashed with monosyllables. He is so starchy and censorious that I knew I could not please him whatever I said," Jane added guiltily, "so I did not mind my tongue as I know I ought."

"Oh, Jane!"

"Dear Gracie, as you yourself said, no one knows you are my governess, so no one will blame you for my shocking lack of conduct. Look, there is a little drawer in this table, and a chess set within. Shall we play a game?" She took out the box of pieces and began to place them on the inlaid squares on the table top. They were beautifully carved in red and yellow wood in the form of Chinese warriors.

"I wonder whether we ought not rather to retire, since we are being ignored with such determination," said Miss Gracechurch uneasily.

"Fustian! I do not mean to be intimidated, I assure you. Besides, Mr. Selwyn and the others will not ignore us when the gentlemen finish their port and join us." Also, she admitted to herself, she was not averse to another skirmish with My Lord Winter. "There, I have given you the white so the first move is yours." Miss Gracechurch, with more experience and more patience, generally won their games, so Jane concentrated fiercely. The gentlemen came in when she was pondering a move, so she did not look up until her bishop—a Buddhist monk—had dashed across the table to rescue a mustachioed warlord of a knight.

Mr. Selwyn had come straight over to them. "Do you object to an observer?" he enquired. "I promise not to interfere." They welcomed him and he pulled up a chair.

Footmen were setting up a pair of card tables. The Danforths and the Parmenters appropriated one.

"Mr. Reid, do you play whist?" Lady Wintringham demanded.

"N-no, my lady," the shy young man confessed. "Only p-p-piquet."

"I like a good game o' whist," said Mr. Ramsbottom. "It'll be a pleasure to take a hand wi' your ladyship."

The countess blenched, but there was no gainsaying the cotton merchant. "Miss Chatterton, be so kind as to give us a little music," she directed, accepting defeat. "Wintringham will turn the pages for you."

"Pray hold me excused, ma'am," said the earl curtly. "I was about to offer Mr. Selwyn a game of chess. There is a second set—in the library."

Miss Chatterton pouted. "I daresay Miss Brooke will like to play. She cannot often have the advantage of so superior an instrument as your pianoforte, ma'am." Possibly she hoped to embarrass Jane by exposing her deficiencies, for her tone held more malice than generosity.

Everyone looked at Jane. She scarcely noticed, for she was staring at Lady Fitzgerald, now seated beside her sister. Knocking over several chessmen, Jane clutched Gracie's arm. "You were right, ma'am. I believe Lady Fitzgerald is going into labour!"

CHAPTER FIVE

LIKE EVERYONE ELSE in the drawing-room, Edmund stared at Lady Fitzgerald. She was holding her swollen abdomen, looking surprised.

"Send for a midwife," yelped Fitz. "Daphne, you said there was a month yet to go!"

"Oh, Fitz dear, you know I am so bad at numbers," she said placidly as the contraction eased.

"Send for a doctor," shouted her distraught husband, clasping her hands. His own shook.

Edmund took a stride towards the bell pull.

"Unfortunately, the fog precludes sending for any-one." The calm, authoritative voice was Miss Grace-church's. She rose and moved forward. "However, I have considerable experience with childbirth and I see no reason why her ladyship should not be safely delivered. My lord, your agitation can only distress your wife. She must be carried to her chamber."

"I shall carry her," Edmund offered. "Fitz, drink a glass of brandy and pull yourself together, man." Without waiting for a response, he picked up Lady Fitzger-ald as if she were an unwieldy package full of fragile glassware, and headed for the door.

Miss Gracechurch was there before him to open it. As he passed her, she turned her head and said quietly, "Jane?"

Crossing the hall to the stairs, Miss Gracechurch at his side, he heard Miss Brooke saying, "My lady, we must have plenty of clean linen and hot water. Miss Gracechurch's maid, Ella, will know what is needed. She has often worked with us. Pray give orders...."

He started up the stairs, careful not to jar his burden, and heard no more. "That chit...that girl...Miss Brooke will assist you?"

"She is no girl but a woman, and yes, she will assist me." She sounded faintly amused. "I have never found it possible to prevent Jane doing anything she has set her heart on."

"That I can believe, more easily than that you are a midwife, ma'am."

"The neighbourhood where we both have lived is isolated, with neither midwife nor doctor, so I considered it my duty to learn the necessary skills."

"Estimable." Edmund's approval was dubious. Delivering babies was no proper occupation for a lady, however reduced her circumstances.

"I am very glad you did, ma'am," said Lady Fitzgerald with a sweet smile.

"Gad, yes!" When it came to the present situation, he concurred wholeheartedly.

"Poor Fitz is in such a taking," poor Fitz's wife continued. "Will you tell him, my lord, that I shall do very well?"

He looked down at her in surprise. As far as he could remember, she had never before spoken so many words to him at one time, let alone asked a favour. What was more, he had supposed that a woman in labour would be moaning and groaning, not serenely reassuring her husband.

"Of course, ma'am," he promised. "I shall keep him company."

Entering the Fitzgeralds' chamber, he laid her on the bed and, suddenly embarrassed, turned to leave just as Lady Fitzgerald's abigail rushed in.

"Oh, my lady, I knew this would happen," she wailed. "I said you was reckoning the weeks wrong. What'll we do?"

"My good girl, you may safely leave your mistress in Miss Gracechurch's hands."

"Begging your lordship's pardon, but you don't know nothing about it, my lord, being a man. And not even married!"

Before he could utter the blistering rebuke that rose to his lips, he found himself shepherded towards the door by Miss Gracechurch. "I shall deal with the girl, my lord," she said, unruffled. "Her ladyship will be glad to have someone with her whom she knows. Do you deal with the expectant father, if you please." With a smile she added, "Yours is the harder task."

Next moment he was out in the passageway with the door firmly closed behind him.

He went back down the stairs. There was something about Miss Gracechurch that inspired confidence, and the youthful Miss Brooke had also sounded calmly competent. Now he just had to convey his trust to his frantic friend.

The drawing-room door was open, and once more he overheard voices within.

"I must go to Daphne, my lady," cried Lavinia. "She needs me. She will wish for a familiar face. Pray say I may go."

"Out of the question." Lady Wintringham, still at her whist table with a hand of cards, sounded as scandalized as her always measured tone permitted. "No young, unmarried lady ought to know of such things, far less to be present."

"But Miss Brooke..."

"My dear Miss Chatterton," the countess interrupted, "Miss Brooke is no lady."

As Edmund stepped into the room, Lavinia flew across to him. "My lord, how is Daphne? Does she not ask for me?"

He took her hands, liking her better than he had thought possible. "Your sister begged me to tell you that she is as comfortable as can be expected," he lied. "Her abigail is with her and I am certain that Miss Gracechurch is to be relied upon."

Over her head, he caught Mr. Reid's eye. The youth whispered to his friend and the two of them approached.

"Miss Chatterton," said Mr. Hancock with a slight bow, "Reid and I were wondering if you'd be so kind as to give us a spot of music. We both have a fancy to sing a glee or two and we need the pianoforte to keep us on the note."

Silently Edmund blessed them. "An excellent notion," he said. "Fretting will not help your sister, Miss Chatterton. 'In sweet music is such art: Killing care and grief of heart.'"

She gave him an alarmed look and went off with Mr. Hancock. Mr. Reid lingered.

"Shakespeare?" he asked. "I thought so. It don't do to quote Shakespeare to the ladies. Mr. Selwyn took Lord Fitzgerald off to the library, my lord."

"Thank you." Taken aback by the unsought advice, Edmund watched the lanky young man lope over to the pianoforte.

The rest of his guests had not allowed so minor a matter as a woman in labour to interfere with their whist. Danforth, a bottle at his elbow, was redder in the face than ever. He and Cousin Amelia were undoubtedly losing as usual. Edmund's sister Judith never played unless there was a good chance of winning, and her colourless husband was tied to her apron strings.

At the other table, Lady Wintringham was in a good humour, discernable only to those who knew her well. Her unlikely partner, Mr. Ramsbottom, must be an excellent player. Though indifferent to the money involved, her ladyship liked to win, yet she would not permit the Tuttles to lose deliberately, as they were all too willing to do. The vulgar Ramsbottom evidently had hidden depths.

In fact, Edmund thought as he made his way towards the library, he had cause to be grateful to all his unbidden guests. Even the Mail coachman had obliged by driving his vehicle off the road, thus providing medical assistance in time of need.

Miss Neville met him in the hall. "Is there anything I can do to help, Cousin?" she asked timidly.

"Thank you, all is well in hand." Edmund continued on his way.

"But has Lady Fitzgerald any clothes for the baby?" she persisted to his back.

He stopped and turned. "No, you are right, I don't suppose she has. However, I would not have you stay up all night sewing."

"Oh no. But I am sure there is a box of baby clothes laid up in lavender in the attic."

"If you can find it, I shall be most grateful."

"I know just where it is!" Beaming, she trotted off to the stairs.

Recalling his earlier feeling of guilt in her regard, Edmund called after her, "I should like to speak to you tomorrow, Cousin. Shall we say three o'clock, in the library?"

She gave him a frightened nod and scurried up the stairs. He frowned, he had not meant to alarm her, but she was a nervous little woman. No matter, his intentions would be clarified on the morrow. He sent one of the footmen on duty in the hall to carry down the box if she found it.

At last he reached the library. For a moment he thought no one was there, then he saw that Fitz was slumped in one of the big leather chairs by the fire, his head in his hands, an untouched glass of brandy on the small table at his side. Selwyn, the lawyer, was standing at the locked, glass-fronted cabinet where Edmund's most valuable books were kept, peering at the titles.

"My lord," he was saying in an abstracted way, "I do believe Lord Wintringham was correct in thinking that a little brandy will steady your nerves."

Edmund closed the door behind him. They both looked round as the latch clicked. Fitz sprang to his feet.

"Ned, how is she?"

"Lady Fitzgerald charged me to tell you that she will do very well. Indeed, she appeared to be perfectly comfortable, and I have every confidence in Miss Gracechurch."

"I agree." Reluctantly Mr. Selwyn left the books. "Though I met Miss Gracechurch only today, I have spoken with her at some length, confined as we were in the coach, and I find her a thoroughly sensible, competent woman. Miss Brooke, also, I believe to be capable, despite her youth and a certain levity of manner."

A twinkle in the staid lawyer's eye suggested that he regarded Miss Brooke's levity with more indulgence than disapprobation. Edmund unwillingly warmed towards him. Fitz, however, refused to be reassured and began to pace with frantic energy.

Edmund wished he could take his friend for a long gallop. Failing that, he insisted on trying for revenge for his earlier defeat and all three gentlemen repaired to the billiard room. Mr. Selwyn, unfamiliar with the game, declared that he wanted Lord Fitzgerald, the victor, to teach him. Being too good-natured to turn him down, Fitz was distracted from his woes.

There Alfred found them. Miss Brooke had sent him to report on progress, "though there ain't a great deal as yet, my lord," he said apologetically. "First babies often takes their time, the young lady says, but her ladyship is resting comfortable between the pains, and in good spirits."

"Pains!" Fitz groaned. Mr. Selwyn hastened to ask his advice on a difficult shot.

Edmund went over to his valet and murmured, "Thank Miss Brooke for the news."

"A fine young lady, my lord, and kind, too."

"Admirable. How is it that you are her messenger?"

"I took it on meself to make sure the ladies has all they need, my lord, seeing as how her ladyship's housekeeper were grumbling fit to bust about taking orders from strangers."

"Thank you, Alfred. What should I do without you?"

"I'm sure I don't know, my lord," said the valet with the familiarity of many years acquaintance.

He reappeared several times as the night wore on into the small hours of the morning. The gentlemen returned to the library to play endless games of cribbage and *vingt-et-un*. At intervals a sleepy footman came in to build up the fire and replace guttering candles. Then a different footman arrived to draw back the curtains and douse the candles. Outside, the fog was a ghostly, luminescent white.

It was not Alfred but Jane Brooke who entered next. Her honey-coloured hair had escaped its pins to hang in uneven loops framing her tired but exultant face.

"You have a daughter, my lord!"

Jumping up, upsetting the cribbage board, Fitz dismissed this irrelevance. "Daphne—how is Daphne? May I see her?"

"If you come at once, sir. She was very nearly asleep when I left."

Fitz sped to the door. She tucked her arm through his in the friendliest way and started telling him about his child as they went off together.

Edmund watched, trying to ignore a twinge of jealousy. Miss Jane Brooke disturbed his emotions in a way he was quite unused to and strongly objected to. He put her out of his mind and turned to the lawyer with a grin.

"Dare we go to bed?"

Mr. Selwyn grinned back. "I believe we might venture to do so, my lord."

"MAY I OFFER YOU a drop o' port, Miss Ella?"

"Thank you, Mr. Alfred, I won't say no."

"Been a long night. Cheers."

"Cheers. It don't seem so long, though, when there's a babe at the end."

"You're right, it don't, somehow. We'd've been in the suds all right without your lady."

"My... Miss Gracechurch is always ready to lend a hand."

"And that Miss Brooke, a fine young lady, and kind with it, like I was saying to his lordship. A spot more for you, Miss Ella?"

"Not for me, ta all the same, I'm off to bed. What did his lordship say to that?"

"Admirable is what he said. And that's a change of tune, I tell you no lie, for he took agin her from the first."

"Miss Jane c'd win over the Devil himself. Good night, Mr. Alfred, or good morning, I should say."

"Sweet dreams, Miss Ella."

CHAPTER SIX

THE LIBRARY was empty. Jane was beginning to realize how vast Wintringham Abbey was. Since coming downstairs shortly before noon, she had met only the Tuttles and Mr. Parmenter, all in the breakfast room.

She had decided on waking that she was more in need of sustenance than sleep. Now, after satisfying her appetite at the munificent buffet, she wanted to curl up with a book. She looked around the huge library, of which she had caught a glimpse last night, and wondered where to begin. It would take a lifetime to explore the delights gathered on those well-dusted shelves.

Purely by chance, she came across Boswell's *Life of Johnson*. Having found his *Tour to the Hebrides* entertaining, she took down the first volume and retired to one of the cavernous wing-chairs by the fireplace.

A footman came in to poke up the fire, adding coals, and to light a branch of candles on the mantel, for the fog-dimmed daylight made reading difficult. Jane resisted the temptation to chat with him, not wishing to bring down Bradbury's ire upon him. No one else disturbed her, and after a while she kicked off her slippers, tucked her feet under her, and made herself thoroughly comfortable.

Not unnaturally after her busy night, comfort led to drowsiness. She was unaware of the library door opening and the sound of a firm tread on the polished floorboards registered only faintly. The scrape of a chair roused her just enough to think that she ought to sit up straight and put on her shoes, but when silence followed, the effort of moving seemed too great. She fell back on a hope that no one would notice her presence.

A voice startled her into full wakefulness.

"Come in, Judith. Pray be seated. I daresay I need not enquire why you asked to see me."

Lord Wintringham, at his most sarcastic. Jane decided it was too late to beat a retreat.

"I am too agitated to sit down. Edmund, you must help us." That sulky whine was his sister, Mrs. Parmenter.

"Must I?"

"If you do not, we shall be ruined!"

"I doubt it."

"Remember that Henry is not a peer. He has no immunity to arrest for debt. Think of the scandal if he is dragged off to the Marshalsea!"

"I cannot think it likely."

"It is certain, if you will not aid us! Can you bear to see the name of Neville, the name of Wintringham, dragged through the mire?"

"The name dragged through the mire will be Parmenter," the earl pointed out with cold contempt.

"Everyone knows the connexion. People will say you have no family pride, that you are too mean to assist your closest relatives."

"Might I suggest that you sell the rubies you were wearing last night, Judith?"

"They are not paid for," she said resentfully.

"Then if you return them to the jeweller you will be relieved of a considerable part of your obligations. And if you rusticate this spring instead of going up to Town for the Season, no doubt you will manage to come about.''

"Not go to Town! It's all very well for you, you prefer to moulder in the country, but..."

"*My* habits are not under discussion, ma'am. You would do well to look to your own, and your husband's. It is past time you learned to be beforehand with the world. I have no intention of throwing my money at your debts only to allow you to contract new ones."

"But, Edmund, we are at *Point Nonplus!*"

"Not a penny. Now, if you will excuse me, I have work to do."

"You odious, cold-hearted brute! You are well named My Lord Winter. I am ashamed to call you brother." Bursting into tears, Mrs. Parmenter rushed from the room and slammed the door behind her.

Jane knelt on the seat of her chair and peeped over the back. Lord Wintringham was standing behind the desk, his face grim.

"You were not very kind," she said.

He started. "What the devil are you doing here?"

"Eavesdropping," Jane admitted candidly. "I beg your pardon, my lord. I did not intend to, but I was reading and I must have fallen asleep. By the time I woke up you were already bullying Mrs. Parmenter and I thought it best not to interrupt."

"Bullying!" He came round the desk and strode towards her.

She sat down quickly and reached for her shoes. Her head bowed as she tucked her toes into one of them, she said with slightly nervous resolution, "Yes, bullying. You were unconscionably harsh, my lord. Can you spare your sister nothing when you are so wealthy? Or—oh dear—perhaps you cannot afford to help her. Is all this luxury built on a heap of debts? I beg your pardon, sir, but such things are known.''

''My dear Miss Worldly-Wise, I could afford to pay the Parmenters' debts twice over and never know the difference.'' Looking almost amused, the earl dropped into the chair opposite Jane and stretched out his long, muscular legs in their skin-tight pantaloons. ''In fact, I have paid the Parmenters' debts a dozen times already. I give Judith an allowance, as I do all my purse-pinched brothers and sisters, and I pay for my nephews' schooling.''

''Oh.'' Jane was aware that her response to this revelation was inadequate, but she was trying to put on her second slipper unobtrusively. Without success—he watched her every move, his lips quirking.

''My other siblings, I am happy to say, manage to live within the means I provide,'' he went on. ''Unfortunately Judith, though merely the daughter of a younger son and married to a gentleman of modest means, aspires to live up to the glory of having an earl for a brother. Henry is swept along in her wake. If I continue to tow them out of the River Tick at every request, they will never attempt to curb their extravagances.''

''No, I expect you are right. But surely you would not let Mr. Parmenter be incarcerated in debtors' prison!''

''I own I should be surprised to see the bailiffs on their doorstep. Judith is by far too calculating to allow things to come to such a pass. No, I believe she is prevaricating to induce me to frank her in advance, and I cannot abide deceit.''

''But if you are wrong?''

''If Henry were actually hauled off to the Marshalsea, I daresay I might gallop to the rescue, after a few days there had taught him a lesson.''

"I am not sure any lesson would enable him to stand up to his wife. He looks so spineless. Oh!" She clapped her hand to her mouth in horror at where the license she had granted her tongue had led her.

His crack of laughter reassured her—and took her breath away. Relaxed, his haughtily handsome face became devastatingly attractive. The ice in his grey eyes melted and they glinted with mirth. Jane gazed at him entranced, her heart performing a peculiar flip-flop. If only he were always like this!

And then, suddenly uneasy, she remembered that she ought not to be closeted alone with a gentleman. Gracie had impressed upon her that such behaviour was fast, and for a young lady to be considered fast was instant social death.

"Don't look so worried, I shan't clap you in irons for *lèse majesté*. Spineless, you say? I have always thought my brother-in-law closely resembles a boiled codfish."

"Oh yes, not so much spineless as chinless." She beamed at him. After all, she was not, at present, Lady Jane, daughter of the Marquis of Hornby. She was plain Miss Brooke, daughter of no one in particular, and Society would never know of her fast behaviour.

"Am I forgiven for leaving him and Judith to come about by their own efforts?"

"Certainly, but you might have told her in a more civil manner. She is your sister, not a street beggar."

For a horrid moment she thought she had gone too far. His lips tightened and a touch of frost reappeared in his expression. Then he said dryly, "A library beggar, rather. But it is most improper in me to be discussing my family's intimate affairs. What were you reading, Miss Brooke, that sent you to sleep?"

They talked for a few minutes about James Boswell and Samuel Johnson, until they were interrupted by a timid tapping at the door. Lord Wintringham pulled out his watch.

"Three o'clock—my cousin Neville. I am sorry to disturb you, Miss Brooke, but when I arranged to interview my relatives in my library, I had not expected it to become a place of common resort."

"You wish to speak privately with Miss Neville?"

"I do. I promise I shall not bully her."

Jane laughed, levering herself out of the deep armchair. "Then I shall go and see if I can visit Lady Fitzgerald and the baby."

He took her hand and gazed down at her with warmth in his grey eyes. "I have not thanked you yet for your invaluable service to Lady Fitzgerald last night."

"We were glad to be able to help," she said, blushing.

As the library door closed behind her, she put her hand to her hot cheek. What had come over her? She was not given to changing colour like a ninnyhammer, and the earl had merely expressed his gratitude. It must have been the way he looked at her. Who would have guessed that grey could be such a warm colour? His hand had been cool, strong yet gentle. Her own still tingled from the contact.

No wonder young ladies were not allowed to be alone with gentlemen, she thought, if the result was to leave young ladies feeling peculiar all over!

A footman was watching her, with curiosity that changed at once to rigid impassivity when he realized he was observed.

"Pray direct me to the nursery," Jane requested. She would go there first, so that she'd be able to take news of the child to Lady Fitzgerald.

Despite precise directions, it took her some time to reach the nursery, tucked away at the top of a distant wing. There she found Miss Gracechurch instructing the housemaid who had been put in charge of the baby because she had once held a position as nursery maid. She had never been in sole charge of a newborn before, and she was absorbing Gracie's words with wide-eyed anxiety.

Rather than interrupt, Jane went straight to the cradle where the Honourable Miss Fitzgerald was fast asleep in a lace-trimmed gown and cap—Gracie disapproved of swaddling bands. The baby's tiny, dimpled fists pressed to her cheeks. Jane thought her decidedly plain with her snub nose and squashed chin, though she wouldn't have dreamed of saying so. She had yet to see an infant whose looks justified the inevitable admiration, but perhaps it was different when one had children of one's own, at least until they reached an age to be bothersome.

Not for the first time, she vowed to herself that her own children, however bothersome, should never be sent away to a distant estate to be reared by servants. This nursery was far enough, isolated enough, from the more frequented parts of the house.

"Too far," said Gracie as they retraced their steps together. "Lady Fitzgerald has to nurse the child herself until a wet nurse can be hired and it is most unwise to carry so young a babe back and forth along miles of draughty corridors. I wonder whether I ought to speak to the housekeeper or to Lady Wintringham herself about preparing a closer room."

"If you like, I will ask the earl."

"The earl! I hardly think you are on such terms with his lordship as to request his assistance in a matter that is the concern chiefly of the lady of the house."

"I have been talking to him, and I believe he is not so black as he is painted. Indeed, when he forgets how important he is and comes down off his high horse, he is an amazingly agreeable gentleman."

"His high horse? Jane, pray do not..."

"...use my brother's slang—I mean, colloquialisms. I beg your pardon, Gracie dear. But do you wish me to speak to Lord Wintringham, in the King's English, about changing the baby's room?"

"I think not. He might mount again onto his high horse."

Jane giggled and impulsively hugged her governess. "I do love you, Gracie."

"And I you, my dear." Smiling, she touched Jane's cheek lightly before reverting to her subject. "Perhaps it will be best if the Fitzgeralds themselves approach Lady Wintringham."

"They might not care to approach so unapproachable a lady for a favour after setting her household at sixes and sevens already. I know: we shall have Ella ask the advice of his lordship's valet, who was so helpful last night."

"An excellent notion. Now the only remaining question is whether I send a footman to fetch Ella or go to my chamber and ring for her. What a trial it is to live in such vast magnificence, to be sure!"

Laughing, they parted and Jane continued to Lady Fitzgerald's room. Both her husband and her sister were there. The Fitzgeralds were delighted to see Jane, but Lavinia Chatterton seemed uncomfortable. After a few minutes, she crossed to the window, glanced out, and said awkwardly, "I fear you may be stranded here for some time to come, Miss Brooke. The fog is as thick as ever."

Surprised by her overture, and a trifle wary, Jane went to join her. "So it appears," she agreed, looking out at the formless whiteness. "I do not recall ever seeing so dense a fog. The poor coachman cannot be blamed for driving the Mail into a ditch."

"And I cannot be sorry for it, since no one was hurt. What should we have done if you had not arrived so opportunely to help Daphne? I do not know how to thank you, Miss Brooke."

"Pray think nothing of it, Miss Chatterton. Fortune having brought us to where we were needed, what else could we do? Besides, your thanks are due more to Miss Gracechurch than to me, for she is the one with the knowledge and I did no more than to follow her orders."

"I shall thank her too," Lavinia promised, then went on shamefacedly, "I . . . I was not very welcoming yesterday. I hope you will forgive me, and that we can be friends?"

"Of course," said Jane, who considered every acquaintance a potential friend until proven otherwise. "I understand perfectly."

"I don't in general put on such airs. You see, my situation is difficult. My mama and Lady Wintringham say I must try to attract Lord Wintringham's interest. I am prodigious lucky that he is Fitz's friend, for he is a splendid parti, rich and titled, and his conduct in every way irreproachable. And he is even handsome, and not too old, so I have nothing to complain of."

"No, indeed."

"But oh, Miss Brooke, I cannot like him. His manner is so...so contemptuous that he frightens me and I can never think of anything to say to him. Did you know that they call him My Lord Winter? I am not the only one who finds him intimidating. I cannot bear the thought of being married to him."

"Then you must not," said Jane decisively. "Stop trying to attach him and follow your own inclination. I am sure there are other equally eligible gentlemen who will be acceptable to both you and your parents."

"Oh yes, I expect I shall meet dozens, for we are soon to go up to Town for the Season."

Dismayed by this news, Jane didn't ask herself why she had not revealed to Lavinia her discovery that beneath My Lord Winter's shell of ice dwelt a most attractive gentleman.

CHAPTER SEVEN

MISS GRACECHURCH paused in the doorway of the library and looked around the room with envy. It was as impressive as Jane had told her.

One of the greatest disadvantages of her past life at Hornby Castle had been the difficulty of procuring books, which offset the advantage of having a great deal of leisure for reading. What the future held she could not guess. Deciding to make the best of the present, she set off on a tour of exploration.

"Perhaps I might be of assistance, ma'am?" said Mr. Selwyn's quiet voice behind her.

She swung round, smiling. "Sir, I beg your pardon. I did not see you."

"These chairs are admirably designed to hide their occupants. Were you looking for something in particular? I fancy I have fathomed his lordship's system of classification."

"To tell the truth, I am overwhelmed by this *embarras de richesse*. I can imagine wandering around forever, unable to make a choice."

"Then might I suggest that you tell me what you like to read and I will select a few books for you, to reduce the perplexity to manageable proportions."

"To choose between subjects is almost as difficult. I shall rely entirely upon your judgement." She sat down in the chair opposite the one from which he had risen.

"But pray do not bring me some technical treatise on agriculture!"

He laughed. "I promise."

His long face was well suited for laughter, she thought, not at all the dry, fussy look one expected of a lawyer. He was as much the gentleman as Lord Wintringham, and with a gentlemanly ease of manner that the earl could not match. Whatever the future brought—at present it appeared less than promising—she would be glad that she had met Mr. Selwyn.

He brought her a half dozen volumes, setting the stack on the table beside her chair. "Our host is a noted bibliophile," he said, as she picked up the top book and read the title. "He has followed in the footsteps of his uncle, the late Earl of Wintringham, who built up this superb collection."

"You sound as if you have the knowledge to appreciate it."

"I myself am a collector, in a small way, of course. I cannot hope to compete with this library, but I have one or two items I believe his lordship might even consider worthy of his locked shelves." He cast a longing glance at a cabinet in one corner.

"Rare books? I fear I should not understand their value. Jane and I simply enjoy reading."

"If you have taught her that, you have taught her a great deal."

"Taught...I...oh dear!" she said, flustered.

"Forgive me, Miss Gracechurch. I do not mean to discompose you, but I flatter myself I am not an unobservant man. Would I be incorrect in guessing that Miss Brooke is something more than she pretends to be, and that you are her governess?"

"Oh dear!" She dropped the book in her lap and hid her scarlet face in her hands. "It was wicked of me to allow her to continue her masquerade."

"Not wicked," he said firmly, "though perhaps unwise. However, I doubt you could have turned her from her course once she was set in it."

"Very true. Jane is a most determined young woman, besides being inclined to act upon impulse, as you have seen. Pray do not misunderstand me: she is also the sweetest-tempered girl. She is like a daughter to me."

"How long have you been with her?"

"Since she was five years old, and she recently turned twenty."

"Fifteen years! But, my dear Miss Gracechurch, you must have been in the schoolroom yourself."

"Not quite." She smiled at him, pleased by the implied compliment. "It was my first private position after teaching for two years in a school."

"A good position, I assume, since you stayed so long."

"I was exceptionally lucky to find such an agreeable situation." *And shall be even luckier to find another like it,* she thought unhappily. When a young lady made her come-out, her governess's duties were finished. "Jane's parents never interfered in her upbringing. Indeed, we seldom saw them from one year's end to the next. A ruined castle and a small manor house do not suit their consequence, I collect, besides being over far from London."

"Then the credit for her disposition and manners is entirely yours, ma'am. Allow me to congratulate you. She is a charming young lady. You are going to London for the Season?"

"Her first. It has been postponed twice because of mourning for two distant cousins." Her indignation on Jane's behalf and his sympathetic interest overcame her discretion. "*Very* distant cousins. I should not dream of saying this to Jane, but I believe her mother has seized upon any excuse to keep her hidden away. Lady Hornby is too occupied with her own amusements to wish to be troubled with bringing out her daughter."

"Lady Hornby? Even I know of the marchioness's reputation as an accredited Beauty."

"Oh dear, I ought not to have told you her ladyship's name, nor spoken so of her. I am becoming as imprudent as Jane."

"My dear Miss Gracechurch," he said earnestly, "I am gratified by your trust. Every word you have said will be held in utmost confidence."

She shook her head. "I do trust you, sir, but I hardly need exact a promise of silence. It seems Miss Chatterton is also to make her bow to Society this spring, as soon as her sister is recovered from her lying-in. I fear Jane's escapade will inevitably be revealed. I wish that wretched Lord Wintringham had not taken it into his head to treat us as honoured guests!"

AT THAT MOMENT, Lord Wintringham was ready to heartily second Miss Gracechurch's wish.

In order to brood in peace over Miss Jane Brooke's inexplicable ability to loosen his tongue beyond all the bounds of propriety—to the point of criticizing his family to a stranger!—he had retreated to his estate office. Thither Mr. Ramsbottom followed him. Impervious to snubs, sarcasm, and silence alike, the cotton merchant pursued his investigation into the economics of running a large estate with the dogged persistence of a terrier after rats.

In the end, Edmund was forced to escape Ramsbottom by going up early to change for dinner. The defeat rankled, and made him the readier to blame Jane Brooke for her earlier interference.

When he went down to the drawing-room, she and Lavinia were chattering with the young students. She smiled at him. His cold glance erased her smile, but far from being crushed she cocked her head and raised her eyebrows a trifle, contriving to look both perplexed and faintly mocking. With a slight shrug, she turned back to Mr. Reid.

So Miss Brooke cared not a whit for his opinion? Fuming, and feeling somewhat foolish, Edmund joined Fitz, who stood leaning against the mantel with his hands in his pockets, beaming at the world with impartial delight.

"Daresay you noticed," he greeted Edmund, "Lavinia didn't so much as blink an eye when you came in."

Edmund had been far too occupied in attempting to put Jane Brooke in her place to pay any heed to Lavinia Chatterton. "No," he grunted.

"Not going to take a miff, are you? I was sure as eggs you'd be pleased so I encouraged her."

"Encouraged her to cut me?"

"Lord no. To follow Miss Brooke's advice."

"Miss Brooke's! And what precisely did Miss Brooke advise your sister-in-law?"

"Not to set her cap at you only because her mama and your aunt bid her, when she wouldn't want you if she caught you. I mean," Fitz corrected himself hurriedly as Edmund glared at Jane's oblivious back, "I daresay she didn't put it quite like that."

"I shall, of course, be glad to be rid of Lavinia's pursuit," said Edmund, regaining his outward composure with a struggle. And he'd be glad to wring Miss Brooke's neck, he added to himself.

For the next few minutes he was forced to listen to Fitz singing Miss Brooke's and Miss Gracechurch's praises. Daphne was sleeping comfortably and the baby had been removed into the next-door chamber, all due to the kind offices of those two admirable ladies.

"Like to ask your advice," said Fitz at last in a low voice, looking round to be sure no one could overhear. The Tuttles, the Danforths, and Henry Parmenter had all come in, but none approached their host and his friend. "Thing is," he went on, "I want to do something to thank them. It's obvious they're both purse-pinched, but do you think they'd be insulted if I offered them a spot of the ready?"

"Yes, I do!" Though Edmund was quite prepared to condemn Jane Brooke's character on any number of grounds, he had never for a moment supposed her mercenary. In his experience, those who wanted money approached with obsequious flattery or whining complaint. He couldn't imagine Jane lowering herself to either expedient.

On the other hand, payment for services rendered was a different matter from begging. However much he disliked her, he didn't want to deny her the comfort of a few extra coins in her purse while she was searching for a post. "I'll try to devise a way to reward them without offence," he promised Fitz.

Reminded of his sister's attempt to feather her nest at his expense, he decided to take her in to dinner to show he held no hard feelings. When Judith sent word that she had the headache and would not come down, he glanced

around the room. There was not one female in it he
wished to sit next to, a sorry state of affairs in his own
house. In fact, the only one to whom he had no positive
aversion was Miss Gracechurch, so he went to join her,
rescuing her from a detailed exposition of Mrs. Tuttle's
illustrious family tree.

Bradbury announced dinner shortly thereafter, and
Edmund found sardonic amusement in Mrs. Tuttle's
chagrined expression when he offered his arm to Miss
Gracechurch.

To his surprise, he actually enjoyed her company.
They talked about literature. Though she in no way put
herself forward, she expressed her opinions without
apology when they differed. He was forced to defend his
own views, and once or twice even to concede that she
might conceivably be in the right. In her own quiet, restrained way she was as forthright as Jane Brooke.

Jane was at present deep in conversation with Ramsbottom. Edmund recalled her comment that, however
vulgar, the cotton merchant was at least easy to talk to.
He hurriedly refocused his full attention on Miss Gracechurch, noting in passing that young Reid, on Jane's
other side, looked most uncomfortable under assault
from Lavinia's fluttering eyelashes. Apparently the boy's
expertise in proper behaviour towards the ladies was
purely theoretical.

The second course was brought in and Edmund
turned unwillingly to his other neighbour. The absence
of two ladies had unbalanced the numbers; Henry Parmenter's fishy eyes met his and darted away.

"I trust Judith's headache is not too severe," said
Edmund.

"No, no, not at all, nothing to it," gabbled his
brother-in-law. "More of a pet, really. That is, you know

what females are, daresay she does have the headache. Megrims! That's the word I want."

So Judith was sulking, as he'd supposed. After exchanging a few pointless remarks on the continuing fog, both gentlemen fell silent.

Edmund found himself once again watching Jane. She was talking to Reid now, and the youth had lost his hunted look. Surprised by a sudden flash of envy for her effortless skill in putting people at their ease, Edmund tore his gaze away from her animated face. The Earl of Wintringham had no reason to envy a chit bound for a joyless life as a governess.

Lavinia had turned her eyelash barrage on Mr. Hancock, who was better able to defend himself than his bashful friend. He appeared to be enjoying the skirmish and giving as good as he got. Edmund saw that Lady Wintringham had noticed their flirtation. Her frown boded ill for the heedless Lavinia.

Perhaps he should try again to convince his aunt that the Honourable Miss Chatterton had no hope whatever of winning his regard.

Beside him Miss Gracechurch, more reserved but as unaffectedly cordial as Jane Brooke, was now chatting with Lord Danforth. Edmund wondered to what extent she had influenced the younger woman. Obviously they were neighbours and close friends. Alfred had said Miss Gracechurch was an impoverished gentlewoman on her way to visit relatives. Probably Jane's father was a clergyman or some such, who had taken the opportunity to send his daughter to London in the company of a respectable older female. It was odd that neither had mentioned any family, but of course he had not asked. Their antecedents were none of his business.

He caught Jane's eye. She gave him a tentative smile and somehow he couldn't help smiling back.

"I DIDN'T MEAN to get her into trouble." Jane plumped down on the love seat beside Gracie and gazed in dismay at Lavinia, shrinking before the onslaught of the countess's wintry wrath. "I only suggested that she stop chasing the earl, not that she should start flirting with Bob Hancock instead."

"Then you have nothing to reproach yourself with."

"No, but I hope Lavinia does not blame me. To tell the truth, I cannot imagine what she sees in Mr. Hancock. He and Mr. Reid are just boys. Oh dear, she does look miserable. How glad I am that Lady Wintringham takes no notice of me whatsoever."

"We might not exist for all the attention she pays us," Gracie agreed, smiling. "However, I had an interesting discussion with her nephew at dinner. As you said, he is a pleasant companion when he forgets his station."

"If only he were consistent. In here, before dinner, he froze me with a look, then at table he smiled at me in the friendliest way."

"Perhaps he had learned in the interim that you were responsible for Miss Chatterton's change of heart."

"Do you think so? She might have told Fitz—I mean, Lord Fitzgerald—and he might have passed it on. He is the only person who seems comfortable with the earl, and I suspect it is because he is impervious to snubs." She sighed. "Lord Wintringham will no longer have cause to be grateful to me if Lady Wintringham frightens Lavinia into setting her cap at him again."

"Jane!"

"Into resuming her pursuit," she amended. "It is amazing how Derek's phrases stick in my mind when we have seen so little of him since he went away to school, and less since he started spending his holidays with friends. Do you think we will be able to visit him while we are in the South?"

"Eton is not too far from London, but I suspect a schoolboy of sixteen might find a visit from his elder sister and his ex-governess a trifle embarrassing."

Jane's laugh was rueful. "No doubt. Last time he came home to Hornby, he spent much more time with the village lads than with us."

While they reminisced about happy days when young Lord Brooke had been content to keep his sister company, Jane kept glancing at the door. Surely the gentlemen would not linger long over the port after last night's disturbances. She was eager to find out whether Lavinia would simply avoid Mr. Hancock at Lady Wintringham's behest, or go so far against her own inclination as to seek out the earl. The girl sat captive at the countess's side, looking thoroughly cowed.

Plump little Miss Neville, on the other hand, had lost her air of timid apprehension. As Jane had noticed earlier, she was positively bubbling with good cheer, as much as anyone could bubble to whom no one paid the least heed. Jane wanted to ask Lord Wintringham what he had said to his cousin. She hoped Lavinia would not monopolize him.

The earl soon led the gentlemen into the drawing-room. As soon as she saw him, his aunt ordered Lavinia to the pianoforte. "Wintringham will turn the pages for you," she said, as she had the previous evening.

Lavinia stood up and curtsied. "I beg your pardon, ma'am, but I believe I ought to pay my sister a visit."

Fitz lent a hand. "I was just going to ask you if you wanted to go with me. Beg you'll excuse us, my lady."

"If your ladyship desires music," said Jane, "I shall be happy to oblige, if Lord Wintringham will be so kind as to turn the pages."

Though the countess ignored her offer and the earl's tight lips rebuked her presumption, she went to the instrument and began to look through the music. He followed her, probably to voice his rebuke, she thought, but Mr. Reid tugged his friend over to join them.

His lordship's repressive silence soon drove the youthful gentlemen to ask permission to play billiards. This granted, they made their escape, Mr. Reid with a wistful backward glance. In the meantime, Jane found a sonata by Johann Christian Bach that she knew so well as to be able to play it without effort. She quickly sat down and began to play.

At the end of the first movement, he said grudgingly, "You play well, Miss Brooke."

"Well enough, but not too well. Playing the pianoforte is an essential accomplishment for a lady, and I enjoy it when I am not made to practise too often." Encouraged by his smile, she returned his compliment. "You turn the pages well, sir."

That surprised a laugh out of him. "Well enough, but not too well."

"Very well. A desirable, if not essential, accomplishment for a gentleman. Turning a page too soon or too late plays havoc with the rhythm and often destroys a piece altogether."

"You speak from bitter experience?"

"I do. In truth, it is a triumph to persuade *some* people to turn the music at all." She was thinking of her brother. To avoid questions which might lead to her family, she turned the subject to his. "You appear to have triumphed over Miss Neville's low spirits. I sup-

pose it was what you said to her this afternoon that made
your cousin so cheerful?''

''I hope so. I merely assured her that if she prefers
keeping house for her brother to dancing attendance
upon my aunt, my carriage shall deliver her to her
brother's house as soon as she wishes.''

''Splendid. I trust she is willing to wait until the fog
lifts?''

''You are very certain that she has not chosen a life of
luxury and comparative leisure at the Abbey,'' he said
dryly.

Jane cast a meaningful glance at the dowager countess, then attempted diplomacy. ''I expect she is prodigious fond of her brother, and I daresay running a
household, however small, is preferable to being a poor
relation even in luxurious surroundings.''

''I daresay.''

''As soon as I saw her happy face, before dinner, I
knew you must have been kind to her. I did not want Mr.
Ramsbottom to embarrass her again, as he did yesterday at table, so I practically forced him to take me in.''

''I doubt force was necessary. You seem to be on excellent terms with the fellow.''

''He is not difficult to manage, if one goes about it the
right way.''

''You are able to manage anyone, are you not, Miss
Brooke?''

The icy edge was back in his tone. Jane's heart sank.
Did he think that she was ''managing'' him, or did he
simply disapprove of her willingness to be friendly with
all and sundry? He disapproved of so many things.

Suddenly the weight of delayed fatigue crashed down
upon her. She was too tired to deal with his capricious
changes of mood. It was all she could do to close the

pianoforte and stand up. "Forgive me if I don't finish the piece," she said with an effort. "I am very weary."

At once he was all solicitude. "Forgive *me,* my dear Miss Brooke. You must be burned to the socket after staying up all last night with Lady Fitzgerald. I shall order tea immediately."

"Thank you, my lord, but all I want is my bed." With the sketchiest of curtsies in Lady Wintringham's direction, she hurried out of the room.

She was holding back tears. Drat the wretched man with his alternating warmth and coldness! Not that the urge to weep was anything to do with him, of course. It was sheer exhaustion.

CHAPTER EIGHT

JANE'S BALL bounced off one side of the billiard table and rolled with unhurried deliberation across the green baize to plop into the middle pocket.

"Oh, well done." Lavinia clapped her hands.

"No, no," Bob Hancock corrected her. "You're supposed to send the other fellow's ball into the pocket, or at least to hit it on the way. Miss Brooke has just given us three points." He chalked them up on the slate.

"Well, I thought it was very clever," Lavinia insisted, "but thank you for the points, Jane."

"I will not say you are welcome to them," said Jane, laughing, "or Mr. Reid will hit me with his cue."

Distressed, the lanky young man assured her earnestly, "I shouldn't dream of doing such a thing. Why, everyone plays a poor stroke now and then. We are still ahead." He glanced at his friend, who was explaining the rules to Lavinia for the fifth or sixth time, and lowered his voice. "Chiefly because Miss Chatterton cannot understand the game. You are a dashed good player for a novice, Miss Brooke."

"At least I know what I am aiming at, even if I cannot hit it."

"I'm glad you are my partner." The Honourable Mr. Reid gazed at her with patent admiration.

He reminded her of a vexatiously devoted puppy who had once followed her about for days, howling whenever he lost sight of her. Like the puppy, Mr. Reid must be discouraged, but she wasn't sure how. Turning away, she saw that Lavinia was pouting and Mr. Hancock looked exasperated.

Time for a distraction, Jane decided. "I have been wondering," she said, "what you two gentlemen did to be rusticated from the university. Since you don't appear utterly cast down, I suppose it was nothing too disgraceful?"

Mr. Hancock grinned. "That was a famous jape, though I don't suppose my father will agree. I daresay the old man will rusticate me down to Somerset post-haste instead of letting me gather a little Town bronze."

"Mine, too," said Mr. Reid, "but it was worth it."

"Do tell us what you did," begged Lavinia, brightening.

Recalling some of her brother's stories, Jane had sudden qualms. "If the tale is fit for a delicate maiden's ears."

"Nothing in the least indelicate," Mr. Reid protested, shocked. "We sneaked into the dining hall just before dinner..." Mr. Hancock paused. "Oh, hullo."

Fitz's cheerful voice came from behind Jane. "Don't let us interrupt. I wager you put salt in the sugar bowls and sugar in the salt-cellars? That's an venerable old trick."

Jane looked round. Lord Wintringham towered behind his shorter friend, his broad shoulders filling the doorway. His disdainful expression bore witness to an utter lack of interest in the childish antics of undergraduates.

Jane directed a welcoming smile impartially at both noblemen, then turned back to Mr. Hancock. "Is that what you did?" she asked, "switched salt and sugar?"

"No, we snaffled the knives from all the tables..."

"Not spoons and forks, only knives." Mr. Reid elucidated.

"And not all the knives," Mr. Hancock continued. "Reid said it would be funnier if we left one on each table and deuced if it wasn't."

"Instead of not being able to eat at all, everyone came to cuffs over the one knife we left."

Picturing the scene, Jane giggled, as did Lavinia. Fitz let out a shout of laughter. "Dashed clever," he said admiringly.

Lord Wintringham looked bored.

More to provoke him than for any other reason, Jane said, "Do you not think, my lord, that it was particularly ingenious to leave one knife per table? Mr. Reid has an original imagination." She smiled at the youth, who flushed with pleasure at her compliment and tried to look modest.

"A pity he does not apply it to a more worthy cause," said the earl caustically.

"Come now, Ned," Fitz protested. "A harmless lark. Boys will be boys, don't you know." As his friend seemed about to contest this statement, he went on hastily, "Having a game of billiards, were you? I didn't know you played, Lavinia."

"Mr. Hancock has been teaching me, but the rules are monstrous confusing. Will you explain to me, Fitz?"

He blenched but said gamely, "Right you are," and went over to the table to demonstrate, with Bob Hancock's assistance, the various possible strokes.

"And are you too confused by the rules, Miss Brooke?" Lord Wintringham sounded faintly mocking.

"I had an excellent teacher in Mr. Reid, my lord."

"Mr. Reid is a veritable paragon."

"He is kind to take the trouble to explain, and kinder to allow me to play as his partner, since my grasp of the rules has not so far resulted in any degree of skill."

"Practice makes perfect, ma'am. Pray excuse me now, I am looked for elsewhere." With a slight bow he strode off towards the front of the house.

Jane stared after him, exasperated. She had nursed a meagre hope that he might condescend to help her improve her play, she admitted to herself. The more fool she.

She became aware that Mr. Reid was regarding her with something approaching awe.

"How brave you are to stand up to My Lord Winter, Miss Brooke! He makes me shiver in my shoes when he ices up like that."

"He was abominably rude to you. Let us forget him."

Lord Fitzgerald had finished his exposition of the rules of billiards, no more successful than Bob Hancock's effort to judge by his sister-in-law's bewildered expression. However, he challenged the young men and Jane to a game, the three of them against himself and Lavinia.

Jane declined. She had lost interest in billiards. "I have not yet visited Lady Fitzgerald and the baby this morning," she excused herself.

"Daphne will be happy to see you," Fitz assured her.

She hurried to the entrance hall, then dawdled up the stairs, but there was no sign of Lord Wintringham. Not that she was sure what she wanted to say to him, if she had met him.

EDMUND LEFT the billiard room in a fit of pique. Jane's praise of Reid had annoyed him, he wasn't sure why.

Except that it had been excessive: the fellow was no more than an irresponsible boy, unworthy of the high regard in which she held him. Yes, a boy, too young for her and too young to be taken seriously.

Wishing he had stayed to give her a few tips on handling her billiard cue, he repaired to his library. There he found the lawyer, Selwyn, once again peering longingly into the locked cabinet.

"My lord, is that... can that possibly be Malory's *Morte d'Arthur* in Caxton's first edition of 1485?"

"Yes. You know it?" asked Edmund, surprised and impressed.

"I know *of* it. I have never seen a copy. There are no more than two or three extant, I believe."

"It's the prize of my collection. Would you like to look at it?"

He extracted the key from the secret drawer in his desk, opened the cabinet, and took out the precious volume, handling it with the utmost care. As he set it on the long table, he dismissed a momentary qualm. Any gentleman knowledgeable enough to recognize the book would know how to treat it, and Selwyn's awed eagerness proclaimed him a confirmed bibliophile.

Some time later Miss Gracechurch entered the library. Edmund half rose to his feet. Selwyn, with More's *Utopia*—the English translation of 1551—in his hands, looked up and smiled absently.

"Pray do not let me disturb you, gentlemen," said Miss Gracechurch. "I have come to return this book, my lord. May I borrow another?"

"Of course, ma'am."

Apparently she knew just what she wanted and where to find it, for a moment later she departed without further interrupting their conversation. *A sensible woman,* thought Edmund.

The lawyer spoke of his own small collection. "My most valuable acquisition is Francis Bacon's *Advancement of Learning,*" he said.

"The first edition? 1605, is it not? I should like to see it."

"I shall be more than happy to show it to you, my lord, if you will do me the honour of calling upon me in Hart Street when you are in Town. Hart Street, Bloomsbury Square."

"Bloomsbury Square. Let me write it down before I forget." But even as he crossed to the desk and made a note, Edmund knew he would not forget Mr. Selwyn's direction. The chance to talk to another book-lover was too rare.

JANE WENT UPSTAIRS to see Lady Fitzgerald and her baby daughter, both flourishing. On her way back down, she made a detour through the long gallery where portraits of the Neville family were displayed, the earliest dating from Tudor times. Miss Neville was there before her.

"I am just bidding my ancestors farewell, Miss Brooke," she explained, her plump face beaming. "Like you, I shall leave the Abbey as soon as the fog lifts. Are you interested in the family history?"

Jane was more interested in the family character, as revealed, she hoped, by their painted faces. However, she didn't want to disappoint the little lady. "Pray tell me, ma'am," she invited.

"It is an ancient lineage, my dear," she said proudly. "Much older than most of the English nobility. There was an Earl Neil of Wintringham before the Norman Conquest.''

"Ancient indeed!'' Jane's first noble ancestor had owed his viscountcy to Charles II's fondness for his wife, and the marquisate had been a reward for supporting George I's claim to the British throne.

"We have no portraits from that period, alas, but the descent can be traced. Under William the Conqueror, the title went into abeyance, the name was Frenchified to Neville, and the greater part of the lands was given to the Roman church to found an abbey.''

"Then I wager the family fortunes revived under Henry VIII.''

"Quite right, my dear. The Dissolution of the Monasteries returned Wintringham to the Nevilles, and King Henry restored the title. Here is the first Earl of Wintringham of modern times.''

The painting was darkened with age, and a full beard curled down across the earl's bejewelled chest, but Jane recognized the square, determined chin. There was nothing of icy hauteur in the Tudor nobleman's gaze, though. He looked to be as full-blooded as his royal master.

As they moved along the gallery, she saw hard faces and weak faces, stern, merry, and even cruel faces, yet none showed the cold disdain so characteristic of Edmund Neville, the present Lord Wintringham.

"Here are my cousins, the late earl and his brother.'' Miss Neville halted before the next to last portrait, in which two young men with powdered hair stood cradling shotguns, hunting dogs at their feet. "You may have noted a more recent painting of the late Lord Wintringham in the drawing-room?''

The irresolute, rather vague, face was familiar. Jane studied with more interest the second young man, who must surely be Edmund's father. Though he had the unmistakable strong Neville chin, his expression was open, cheerful, even friendly. How had he produced so aloof a son?

"And the present Lady Wintringham." Miss Neville's tone was full of resentment. "We need not linger over her, she is not even a Neville by birth, of course. The daughter of a mere baronet, and a second baronet, at that." She sniffed disparagingly.

In her late twenties, the present Lady Wintringham had been a strikingly handsome woman, but even then her beauty was marred by her air of arrogant contempt. The children grouped about her, three girls and a boy of eight or so, were already marked with the same trait.

Edmund Neville was no blood relation of the countess, yet she was undoubtedly responsible for the characteristics that had earned him the sobriquet "My Lord Winter."

Puzzled and curious, Jane followed her guide out of the gallery. She wasn't sure what questions to ask, and she hesitated to interrupt Miss Neville's explanation of her own relationship to the family. They reached the drawing-room, and the opportunity to learn more of Lord Wintringham was gone.

A number of people had gathered in the long room, reading, writing letters, sewing, or conversing quietly. His lordship was not among them, nor his aunt, but Gracie was there.

"What are you reading, ma'am?" Jane asked her. "I left my book in the library, I think."

"If you go to fetch it, try not to interrupt the gentlemen. They are absorbed in studying some musty old volumes." Miss Gracechurch sounded unwontedly disgruntled but Jane scarcely noticed.

"Lord Wintringham is there? I shall not disturb him if I can help it. We are at daggers drawn at present."

"Oh Jane, what did you say to him?"

"I? Nothing! He is as changeable as a weather vane, I vow. I shall go for my book and see whether he has recovered his temper."

When Jane entered the library, the earl was locking the doors of the glass-fronted cabinet while Mr. Selwyn thanked him for a rare treat. The lawyer saw her and asked if she knew where Miss Gracechurch might be found.

"In the drawing-room, sir. She is reading. I came to find my book." Jane circled the table and went to check the stand beside the chair where she had been sitting.

"The *Life of Johnson,* Miss Brooke?" enquired Lord Wintringham.

"Yes, sir." She was astonished that he had remembered. "I left it in here, I believe, but it is gone."

"No doubt it has been reshelved."

"Heavens, I shall never find it again!"

He laughed. "I daresay I might lay hands upon it for you, but perhaps you would be kind enough to indulge me with a game of chess?"

Jane accepted with alacrity. Since his discussion with Mr. Selwyn had dispelled his ill humour, she had no intention of wasting a moment of his agreeable mood. Then, as he took a chessboard from a drawer in the table, she realized that the lawyer had departed.

Once more she was alone with the earl. Her heart began to thud within her chest and her breathing felt strange. "Sh-shall we play in the drawing-room?" she suggested, her voice strangled. She cleared her throat.

"The Chinese chess set is so delightful, I should like to play with it again."

"As you will, ma'am." Closing the drawer, he gave her a questioning glance, as if he was aware of her discomposure. "Let me get your book for you so that you don't have to search for it later."

"Thank you, my lord." She moved to the door while he went straight to the correct shelf and brought her the volume.

Crossing the hall to the drawing-room, they sat down at the little chequer-board table and set out the pieces. Gracie was talking with Mr. Selwyn, and Lady Wintringham had joined Miss Neville and Mrs. Tuttle.

"Chess is such an intellectual game, I vow," said Mrs. Tuttle in a carrying tone. "I have always considered it most unsuitable for delicately bred females, do not you, ma'am?"

"Indeed, only a bluestocking would care to try it," her ladyship agreed. "No female can expect to play well enough to challenge a gentleman, but doubtless Wintringham will permit Miss Brooke to win."

"I hope you will not, sir," said Jane with low-voiced indignation. "I had rather lose honestly than win by default."

He smiled at her. "Never fear, Miss Brooke, I shall consider it an honour to defeat a bluestocking."

"You are very confident!"

"Not, I promise you, because you are a female, but because I have several years' more experience."

"That is true," she conceded, moving a pawn forward. "Besides, I am not really a bluestocking."

His smile broadened to a grin. "Are you not? Pray don't tell my aunt. She will be sadly disillusioned."

"I would not disappoint her for the world." In a louder voice, she continued, "Chess is thought to be of Indian origin, is it not, my lord?"

"I believe the game was introduced into China from India, though it may be of Persian origin. Certainly, in this set the pieces we would call bishops appear to be Buddhist monks, and Buddhism is an Indian religion, not Persian."

Jane knew next to nothing about Persia and not much more about China. She steered the conversation to Indian beliefs and customs, having read two or three books on the subject when the Hornby vicar's son had gone off to India to make his fortune. The earl gravely followed her lead, a smile lurking in his eyes. She knew he was as conscious as she was of Lady Wintringham's ill-hidden satisfaction in hearing her opinion of the upstart Miss Brooke borne out.

Her ladyship's frosty face almost cracked in a smile when her nephew declared checkmate after an unequal struggle.

"You were not concentrating," Lord Wintringham consoled Jane *sotto voce*. "You were too busy convincing my aunt of your bluestocking credentials."

"Yes, but you would have won anyway. You are by far the better player. If we were to stay here longer, I should ask for lessons."

"Who knows, perhaps the fog will persist for a fortnight."

Did he sound hopeful? With regret, Jane dismissed the possibility.

CHAPTER NINE

"THE FOG'S THINNING, MY LORD."

Edmund strode to the window of his dressing-room and pulled aside the curtain. The haloed moon shone down through a thin curtain of swirling mist. "So it is, Alfred." He strove to keep the disappointment out of his voice.

Apparently he succeeded. "'Spect you'll be glad to see the back o' that lot," said his valet gloomily. "The Mail coachman already went off to arrange to pick 'em up tomorrow."

"You don't sound pleased."

"The truth is, I've taken a proper fancy to Miss Gracechurch's maid, my lord." He sighed as he poured hot water into the basin on the washstand. "Well, there ain't no future in it, and that's a fact."

"Perhaps you'll be able to see her in Town. Why don't you ask for her direction?" For some reason, the thought cheered Edmund.

Alfred also brightened. "I'll do that, my lord. We'll be going to London, then?"

"I have some business that will take us up at some point this spring. In April, perhaps. Will Miss Grace-church be there so long?"

"I dunno. Acsherly, I don't even know if she'll be staying in Town or going on somewhere else. Ella don't happen to have mentioned it."

"Well, find out, man." His spirits sank again. Even if Miss Gracechurch were to take up residence in London, her young friend might find a position anywhere in the country. Not that Miss Jane Brooke's situation affected him in the slightest, except that he felt it a pity such a lively damsel should be destined to become a governess.

Alfred was helping him into his coat when Fitz knocked on the door and came in.

"The fog will be gone by morning," he announced. "My man tells me the Mail coachman has already gone to report the accident."

"So I understand. Doubtless he will return with another vehicle to pick up his passengers."

"Miss Gracechurch and Miss Brooke will be leaving. You said you'd think up a way to reward them for helping Daphne. Any ideas?"

"The more I see of them, the more certain I am that to offer money would offend them." Edmund pondered a moment. "I suggest you lend your carriage to carry them to London. They will travel in far greater comfort and avoid incidental expenses along the way."

Fitz beamed. "That's a devilish good notion, Ned. I'll give my coachman enough blunt to pay the reckoning for their meals and such."

"He will be able to tell you where they are staying, and perhaps when you go up to Town you'll discover further ways to assist them." He affected not to see Alfred's wink and broad grin. No doubt his valet also would extract Miss Gracechurch's—and her maid's—direction from Fitz's coachman.

"Yes, I daresay Daphne will be able to help Miss Brooke find a good post," said Fitz with satisfaction.

"The fog's nearly gone, Miss Jane."

"Oh no, is it?" Jane sped to her chamber window and parted the curtains. A bright star twinkled down at her and not far off the winter skeleton of a tall beech stood wreathed in moonlit veils of mist. "Bother! I suppose we shall have to leave tomorrow."

"Don't you want to, my lady?" Surprised, Ella reverted to her mistress's title. "Miss, I mean. I thought you was that keen to get to London."

"I was. I am. But not when My Lord Winter is just beginning to thaw. He was agreeable all afternoon."

Agreeable to Jane, at least. He had thoroughly snubbed the impervious Ramsbottom and poor, sensitive Mr. Reid. She suspected he did not do it deliberately, with intent to hurt. His usual manner was enough to rebuff most people. She had hoped that, given another few days, she might persuade him to adopt a less freezing demeanour.

She said as much to Gracie when she joined her in her bedchamber.

"My dear, a man's nature is not so easily changed."

"I don't believe he is cold by nature. It's more like a suit of armour he puts on."

"To protect himself from the world?"

"To keep the world at a distance, rather. Armour is the wrong word."

"If he wishes to keep the world at a distance, no doubt he has his own reasons. You had best not interfere, Jane."

"I shall have no opportunity, since we must leave tomorrow," she said discontentedly.

They went down to the drawing-room. Fitz rushed up to them, his good-natured face complacent.

"Ladies, allow me to offer my carriage to take you to London tomorrow."

"You are very eager to see the last of us, my lord," Jane teased.

"No, no, nothing of the sort, I assure you. In fact, I left Lavinia moaning to Daphne that she won't know how to go on without you, Miss Brooke. You see," he added in a low voice, glancing behind him, "being confined to her bed, Daphne won't be able to support Lavinia against all the other females as you have."

"Lady Fitzgerald will soon be up and about," Miss Gracechurch assured him. "She is rapidly recovering her strength."

"Do you think so, ma'am? By Jove, I wish you was staying. Dash it, you need not leave so soon after all. My carriage can take you any time."

Jane looked hopefully at Gracie, but that lady shook her head. "We must not trespass on Lady Wintringham's hospitality, sir."

"Lord, I should say not. It don't bear thinking of. You will accept my carriage, though, won't you? I shan't be going anywhere till Daphne's fit to travel—and my cattle need the exercise," he added with an air of inspiration.

This time Gracie nodded and Jane said, "You are very kind, my lord. We shall be glad to accept."

"Good, that's settled then. I'll go and give my coachman his orders right away. Ten o'clock suit you? It's four or five hours' drive, so you will arrive in broad daylight."

As Fitz went off to find his coachman, a sudden thought struck Jane. Aghast, she turned to Gracie.

"But if his carriage takes us to St. James's Place, everyone will know who I am!"

"So we shall not go directly to your father's house, my dear. We can go to an inn or, if you have no objection, we might take up Mr. Selwyn and hire a hackney from his house."

"Will he not think it odd?" Jane said doubtfully.

Miss Gracechurch blushed. "I fear he already knows your secret. He guessed the greater part and I...I trusted him with the rest. He will not give you away."

Before Jane could respond, Lord Wintringham came towards them. "I hope you have accepted the offer of Fitz's carriage," he said. "I should have lent you mine but that it is already promised to my cousin Neville."

Jane gave Gracie a triumphant glance. His lordship, she felt, had proved that his nature was amiable. "Thank you, sir," she said, "we are to go in Lord Fitzgerald's carriage. Do you suppose he would mind if we invited Mr. Selwyn to travel with us?"

"Mr. Selwyn? I cannot imagine that Fitz will object, but I trust you do not mean to pile the rest of your fellow-passengers on the roof."

Laughing, Jane assured him that the thought had crossed her mind, only to be reluctantly dismissed.

Lavinia came in, followed by the two students. She began to bemoan Jane's departure. "I wish we could go, too," she complained. "Daphne is perfectly well. I am sure she is fit to travel."

"Not for at least a fortnight," said Miss Gracechurch firmly.

"Then Fitz could take me to Town now and come back to fetch Daphne later."

The earl withered her with a contemptuous query: "You would leave your sister alone, and confined to her chamber, in a household you find uncongenial?"

Crimson-cheeked, Lavinia flounced off on Bob Hancock's arm. Lord Wintringham's amiability was not to be relied upon, Jane reflected.

Though uneasy in his lordship's presence, Mr. Reid lingered. "I wish I had purchased an inside seat," he murmured wistfully to Jane, "but at least we shall meet at the inns."

"I fear not." She explained to him about Fitz's offer. He looked so disappointed, she patted his arm consolingly. Lord Wintringham frowned.

Mr. Reid's expression denoted an internal struggle. Jane suspected a conflict between his strict notions of the proper behaviour towards ladies and a desire to ask for her direction. She could not tell him, yet she did not want to snub him, so she started talking about the route to London. She had heard that Henley was a very pretty place, and she longed to view the magnificent prospect of Windsor Castle, of which she had a woodcut at home.

"It is visible from the turnpike road, is it not?" she asked the earl.

He assured her that it was visible, and impressive, from a great distance. At that moment, Lady Wintringham entered the drawing-room. Jane at once asked an earnest question about the history of the castle. She could tell by the amused gleam in his lordship's eye as he answered, at length, that he knew she was doing her best to keep up her character as a bluestocking.

He took her in to dinner. Mr. Reid succeeded in seating himself on her other side, and during the second course he did his best to manoeuvre her into disclosing where she was to stay in Town, without asking outright. She out-manoeuvred him with ease, diverting the conversation to the amusements of the metropolis.

As she expected, his tastes ran to such entertainments as Astley's Amphitheatre, steam-boat rides on the Thames, and balloon ascensions. Jane hoped—silently—that she would have time between balls and routs to enjoy such pleasures.

When she turned back to Lord Wintringham, she found him sombre. This she put down to his other neighbour, his sister, who was still in the sulks. However, he failed to respond to her overtures, so she finished her meal in discouraged silence. Their relationship had returned to its initial state. Then, at that first dinner, she had forced him to talk to her. Now, she could not bring herself to make the effort. After tomorrow she would never see him again.

Or if she did, it would be to suffer his anger at her deception.

She was almost glad when, after dinner, Lavinia demanded her company in playing duets. Fitz, Reid, and Hancock gathered around the pianoforte. Lord Wintringham took himself off to his library.

"YOU HAVE PACKED UP all your ladies' clothes already, have you, Miss Ella?"

"Aye, there weren't much, seeing as you can't take much on the Mail."

"You'll be travelling in style this time, in Lord Fitz's carriage."

"I liked it fine on the roof of the Mail. Cold, right enough, but you get a grand view, and atween the coachman and them two young gentlemen we had a lively time of it."

"Did you, now! I wish you wasn't going, Miss Ella. I'm going to miss you, and that's the truth."

"Well, now, I don't say as I won't miss you too, Mr. Alfred. Ever so kind and helpful, you've been."

"My pleasure, I'm sure. You know what—his lordship says we'll be going up to Town sometime. I'd like fine to see you again."

"Get on with you!"

"I tell you no lie. Your Miss Gracechurch wouldn't mind you walking out with me, would she?"

"That's as may be, Mr. Alfred."

"Go on, give us your direction, girl."

"Lor, I couldn't do that, not for the world."

"Why not? Aren't I good enough for you?"

"Plenty good enough, and I'm not saying I wouldn't like to see you, but... Tell you what, you give me your direction and maybe I'll get in touch one of these fine days."

"Wintringham House, in Grosvenor Square. Just leave a message with the butler. He's starchy as old Bradbury but he'll see I get it. Promise you will?"

"I'm not promising nothing, and it's no good looking Friday-faced."

"I won't look Friday-faced no more if you'll give me a kiss, Ella."

"My, hark at the saucy fella! Well all right, Alfred, but just one, mind, and watch out for my tatting."

THE EARL DID NOT APPEAR in the breakfast room while Jane was there. She refused to believe he would not say goodbye. Nonetheless, as she went upstairs to put on her cloak she tried to think of an excuse to seek him out.

The excuse lay waiting for her, in the shape of the book on the dressing-table. It must be returned to the library, and of all places in the vast house his lordship was most likely to be there.

Quickly donning the brown cloak, she hurried down again. The library was empty, even when she checked the deep, concealing chairs by the fireplace. Disconsolate, she set the book on the table and wandered over to the window. She had seen nothing but fog from it before, but now she discovered that it overlooked the broad sweep of drive in front of the wide marble steps up to the front door.

A sound behind her made her turn round, hopefully. Mr. Reid approached her with tentative steps, his gangling form rendered more solid by the three capes of his greatcoat.

"The coach will be here any minute," he said. "Miss Brooke—Jane—I *must* see you in London."

"I'm sorry, it's impossible."

"But I don't care if you're going to be a governess. I love you!"

To her astonishment, he clumsily enveloped her in his arms and bent his head, his lips pursed, with the evident intention of kissing her. She turned her head and the inexpert kiss landed on her temple. Her face buried in his lapel, she uttered a muffled protest.

He squawked and released her. Lord Wintringham had him by the collar.

"Well, really!" Jane would have delved into her memory for some of her brother's choicer epithets if the earl had not been present. "I must say I had thought better of you, Mr. Reid. You ought to be ashamed of yourself."

His face scarlet, he stammered a contrite apology. His lordship, looking grim, let go, and he fled from the library.

Jane's indignation gave way to embarrassment. "Very young gentlemen can be such nodcocks," she said uncertainly.

"You prefer experience?" The earl's strong arm encircled her waist, his hand raised her chin, his enigmatic grey eyes penetrated, dominated her will, held her motionless and robbed her of breath. His mouth descended on hers, hot, demanding, insistent.

She melted in his embrace, clinging to his broad shoulders. He loved her! Her doubts, her perplexity, her misgivings about his character began to fade like will-o'-the-wisps in the sunlight.

Feather-light, his kisses caressed her cheek and fluttered across her brow. He pulled her closer, crushing her against his hard-muscled body. A fire ignited within her—and alarm awoke.

"No!" No, he didn't love her. He thought she craved his familiarities, preferring the attentions of a wealthy earl to those of a green boy scarce loosed from his mother's apron-strings. She had forgotten that to him she was no lady, just an unprotected girl with her way to make in the world. "No!" she cried again, and wrenched herself from his arms.

He made no attempt to detain her. As she tried to pin up her dishevelled hair, he stood watching her, his gaze brooding.

"I ought to scream," she said in a shaky voice, "or swoon, or slap your face."

His lips, so lately tender, curled in contempt. "Why don't you?"

She swung away from those piercing eyes. Outside the window, a travelling carriage with crested doors was pulling up before the steps.

"Lord Fitzgerald's carriage." Gathering the shreds of her tattered dignity about her, Jane raised the hood of her cloak and stalked towards the door, saying haughtily as she went, "*Some* gentlemen of *all* ages never reach the age of reason."

Had she glanced behind her, she might have been surprised by My Lord Winter's wryly troubled smile.

CHAPTER TEN

"YOU HAVE GROWN monstrous tall, I vow. A regular maypole." The Marchioness of Hornby regarded Jane with a moue of distaste. Herself a golden-haired pocket Venus, she had for half a decade laid claim to the nine-and-twenty years she had in fact attained a full decade ago. A daughter of twenty, even if passed off as eighteen, was going to be a sore trial to her.

Beside her mother's delicate porcelain prettiness, Jane felt like a clumsy giant. Lady Hornby's frivolous boudoir, all pink and white with silver frills and gauzes, augmented her discomfort. Thank heaven her own hastily prepared apartments, while elegant, were more staidly furnished.

"Well, your height cannot be helped," her ladyship continued fretfully, "but something will have to be done about your hair and those distressing clothes. If I am obliged to present a daughter to the ton, at least she must be presentable. Your abigail must be turned off and I shall find you a competent dresser."

"I cannot dismiss Ella! Her family has been employed at Hornby forever."

"Then send her back to Hornby."

Jane decided that pleading her maid's hurt feelings would not impress the marchioness. "No, I want her with me," she said with determination. "She will soon learn, Mama."

"Oh very well, but I beg you will not call me 'Mama'. It is so very aging, I vow. I daresay people would stare if you used my Christian name, so you may simply address me as 'ma'am'."

"Yes, ma'am," she agreed unhappily. My Lord Winter's iciest gaze had never chilled her as did her mother's words. By now she was convinced that had she not taken matters into her own hands she'd have waited in vain for a carriage to fetch her from Lancashire.

"Pickerell, send for the *friseur* and the modiste," Lady Hornby ordered her dresser, without so much as glancing at the tall, gaunt woman. "If Lady Jane is to be made ready for her come-out ball they must be put to work at once."

"I am to have a ball, Ma . . . ma'am?"

"La, of course, you silly child. And to be presented at Court. It is expected. I shall have to be hostess for the ball and chaperon for your presentation, so the sooner they are over with the better."

"But will you not chaperon me throughout the Season, ma'am?" Jane asked, bewildered but ready to fight any attempt to send her back to Hornby.

"And be constantly explaining that you are my daughter? That would be the outside of enough! It will not be difficult to find someone to take you about."

"I have a number of aunts, have I not?"

"Yes, but unfortunately they either live abroad, married to diplomats or soldiers or East India officials, or they are ridiculously preoccupied with young families in the country. I expect I shall have to hire someone. Your governess, for instance—what is her name?"

"Miss Gracechurch."

"Gracechurch is a well-bred female, is she not?"

"Oh yes, ma'am, and elegant."

"Then doubtless she will prove suitable. I'm sure I cannot waste much time on the matter. Now off you go. I am obliged to attend one of Hornby's tedious political dinners tonight and it is time to dress. You may come and see me again when your head is fit to be viewed and you have had a few fashionable gowns made up."

Jane curtsied and went out into the gas-lit hallway. Her elation at the prospect of having Gracie for her chaperon contended with the hollow hurt of her mother's lack of pleasure in her arrival and interest in her future.

She was desperate to see Gracie, but she had no idea where to find her. Though nowhere near as vast as Wintringham Abbey, the St. James's Place mansion was spacious for a Town house. Jane's rooms were at the back; arriving in the dusk, she had caught a glimpse from her windows of a walled garden, and beyond it Green Park with its herds of cattle and deer.

Crossing the landing at the top of the stairs she saw that a maroon-liveried footman stood there at call, the same tall young man who had fetched her to her mother's boudoir. As she spoke to him, she wondered what had become of her own Thomas, and old Tom Coachman.

"Do you know where Miss Gracechurch's chamber is?" she asked.

"Yes, my lady. Will I fetch miss to your ladyship?"

She looked at him in surprise. The thought of summoning her governess like a servant had never crossed her mind. "No, pray direct me thither."

"'Tis the servants' quarters, my lady," he said dubiously. "'Tain't fitting..."

"I shall judge what is fitting. Show me the way."

He led her up a pair of back stairs to a narrow, carpetless corridor lined with doors at close intervals. At least they were not quite in the garrets. These must be the upper servants' rooms, the housekeeper and butler, her ladyship's dresser, his lordship's secretary and valet . . . and Gracie. The footman knocked.

"Who is it?"

"It's Jane!" She burst into the small, drab room. "Oh, Gracie, I didn't know they had tucked you away in a horrid corner. This will never do. I shall speak to the housekeeper at once."

With an effortful smile, Miss Gracechurch gestured at the window by which she stood. "I have a view of the park, Jane, and the room is not uncomfortable. You must not upset your mama's arrangements."

"I don't believe Mama—whom I am to call ma'am!— cares a fig where you are lodged. Besides, as you are to be my chaperon, you ought to be close to me at all times."

"Your chaperon?"

"The marchioness does not care to be seen with her daughter at her heels. So shockingly aging!"

"My dear!"

"I don't care, Gracie," said Jane defiantly. "I had much rather have you with me. You will not refuse?"

"Of course not, my dear child. For my own sake, as much as for yours. I had expected the marchioness to give me notice."

"Never! Whatever should I do without you?" She ran into Gracie's welcoming arms and hugged her, her throat tight.

Together they went down to Jane's chamber, where Ella was unpacking her trunk. Thomas and Old Tom, she announced, had arrived the previous day, having avoided the fog by taking the stage via High Wycombe rather than Henley. No one in the house seemed interested in the fact that the party from Lancashire had arrived in two separate groups.

Jane sent for the housekeeper, a colourless but efficient woman who apologized stiffly for her mistake. In no time Miss Gracechurch was established in a nearby guest chamber and a maid instructed to wait upon her.

The two ladies dined before the fire in Jane's sitting-room, a pleasant apartment decorated in pale blue and green enlivened by painted and embroidered posies of bright yellow flowers. As Thomas, delighted to see his mistress again, served them the delectable concoctions of the French chef, they made plans for the morrow.

"At last I can believe I shall really have a Season," said Jane with a contented sigh.

That night, too excited to fall asleep, she found the memory of her mother's petulant face haunting her. She dismissed it firmly, only to have it replaced by the haughty, handsome features of the Earl of Wintringham. The contemptuous twist of his mouth changed to a smile of sardonic amusement, his hostile gaze warmed to tenderness. She felt again the disturbing pressure of his arm about her waist, the touch of his lips...

"No!" As she had then, she cried the word aloud, sitting up in bed and covering her face with her hands. He had taken unconscionable advantage of her inexperience. She was determined to forget him.

A WEEK PASSED in a flurry of activity. The dressmaker came to take Jane's measurements and suggest styles and colours and fabrics. The *friseur* came, and was forced, like Ella before him, to admit that Jane's hair simply would not take a curl; however, he suggested a new way of dressing it in soft loops that pleased her. And then there were endless shopping expeditions, shopping for shawls and reticules, slippers and bonnets, parasols and fans, ribbons and gloves and stockings.

Jane made sure that Miss Gracechurch obtained her share of this bounty.

"How mortifying it would be to have my chaperon looking like a governess," she teased. "That lavender silk will become you admirably, and now we must find you a pelisse and bonnet to match."

Even Ella had two new gowns, "Just so's that hatchet-faced Pickerell female can stop looking down her nose at me afore she goes cross-eyed." She was thrilled with a black silk for everyday wear and a startling lime green that caught her fancy for best. Both she proudly trimmed with lace she had tatted herself.

Though Jane enjoyed the fascinating shops of the metropolis, by the end of a week she was ready for a change.

"Tomorrow," she proposed as Old Tom drove them home from Oxford Street in the elegant Town carriage, "let us walk in Green Park, and take out a subscription at Hookham's Library, and visit Mr. Selwyn. He will think we have forgotten him."

"I cannot think that the marchioness would approve of your visiting a lawyer," said Miss Gracechurch wistfully, her brow wrinkled with worry.

"She will never know. I have only spoken with her three times since we arrived! I realize now you were right to say that Mr. Selwyn must not call on you in St. James's Place, but I promised him I should take you to see him. When we get home, Thomas shall go to Hart Street with a note to see what time will be convenient."

Thomas returned with an invitation to drink tea in
Hart Street the following afternoon. In the meantime,
Jane and Miss Gracechurch had tried on a number of
new gowns which had been delivered while they were
out. Jane thought Gracie looked particularly young and
pretty in a walking dress of amber jaconet muslin with
a Circassian cloth pelisse to match.

"You shall wear that tomorrow," she said, "and Ella
shall dress your hair in ringlets. Mr. Selwyn will scarcely
recognize you!"

She herself wore a pale blue gown with a slate-blue
pelisse. The modiste had assured her that her colouring
was admirably suited to the pastels required for a young
lady, even white, which could be such a trying colour.
The woman had also praised her elegant height and figure. Lady Hornby's strictures were forgotten and Jane
set out with confidence for her first social engagement
since arriving in Town.

Thomas had procured a hackney for them, which
awaited them just around the corner, since a carriage
bearing the Hornby crest would have aroused comment
in bourgeois Bloomsbury. And when they reached the
tall, narrow house in Hart Street, the lawyer's cheerful
elderly housekeeper greeted Jane as Miss Brooke, as she
had requested in her note. If she was not known here as
Lady Jane, surely no gossip could possibly reach her
mother.

Mr. Selwyn welcomed them with delight to his comfortable if unfashionable home. Jane was amused by his
evident admiration of Gracie. That Miss Gracechurch
had also noticed his glances was proved by the delicate
colour that rose in her cheeks, and her reticence as he
settled them in his small sitting-room, inviting her to
pour the tea.

Jane chattered to him about the activities of the past week while Gracie recovered her countenance. Gradually the conversation turned to such subjects as the Royal Academy and the British Museum. It was Jane's turn to fall silent, not from lack of interest but because Mr. Selwyn's company, together with being addressed as Miss Brooke, forced upon her unwanted recollections of Wintringham Abbey.

For a week she had successfully banished My Lord Winter from her consciousness—except for drowsy moments falling asleep or waking when she could not control her memory. Now, against her will, his image rose again to trouble her peace.

However, the next fortnight allowed Jane little leisure to brood over the infuriating earl. That very day, arriving home from Bloomsbury, they discovered that they were to dine with Lord and Lady Hornby, who for once were dining at home without guests. Jane was a trifle nervous, not on her own account but for her governess. Gracie would undoubtedly be blamed if her pupil's conduct fell short of the marchioness's unknown standards of propriety.

She need not have worried; all went well. In fact, as the ladies left him to his port, Jane's father told her kindly, "I believe you will do very well, my dear. Your mother will soon teach you the little nuances of Court etiquette."

Jane curtsied to the tall, thin, stooped gentleman she scarcely knew and gave him a grateful smile. As they left the dining-room, she thanked heaven she hadn't inherited his beak of a nose.

"The Queen's next Drawing Room is in ten days time," announced her ladyship with a martyred sigh. Reclining on a *chaise longue* by the fire and disposing her skirts, a froth of rose-pink *barège,* in elegant abandon about her slim ankles, she went on, "I suppose you have ordered a Court dress?"

"Yes, ma'am. A white silk petticoat over hoops, with an overdress of white lace and a headdress of white feathers. The modiste said that hoops and feathers are *de rigueur?*" she ended on an uncertain note.

"Queen Charlotte's notions of fashion are positively Gothic. I shall have to spend the next few days showing you how to go on at Court, and I daresay I ought to introduce you to a few hostesses since your ball will be three days after the Drawing Room. How tedious!" Diamonds flashed as the marchioness raised a dainty, languid hand to cover her yawn.

"I am very grateful, ma'am." Jane tried to keep the resentment out of her voice. "I shall do my best to be a credit to you and my father."

"Yes, well, tomorrow will be time enough to start. You may retire now, Jane. Your father will go to his club and I am expecting some friends to call."

Reaching the landing halfway up the stairs, Jane heard the doorbell ring and paused to see which of her mother's flock of admirers had arrived. The butler admitted two gentlemen, one a willowy youth dressed with poetic carelessness, the other of middle height and middle years, clad in black, with a dark face ravaged by dissipation. The poet glared at the rake, who ignored him with an air of boredom. They were ushered into the drawing-room.

Jane shook her head in puzzlement. The other *cicisbeos* she had previously glimpsed were a stout, elderly dandy—one of the Prince Regent's set, according to Ella—and a rugged young man of perhaps three-and-twenty who looked like an aspiring Corinthian. She could not understand what pleasure her mother found in their company.

Certainly the marchioness seemed to find little pleasure in her daughter's company. In the days that followed, Lady Hornby instructed Jane in the finer points of Court and Society etiquette; took her to call on the most prominent hostesses, including three patronesses of Almack's; and hired a dancing master to teach her the waltz and the quadrille. All this she carried out without any sign of enjoyment. When Jane mastered the dance steps and the deep curtsy, and was described by no less a Tartar than Mrs. Drummond-Burrell as a pretty-behaved girl, her mother reacted with relief, but neither pride nor praise.

After all the preparation, Queen Charlotte's Drawing Room was an anticlimax. A swarm of young ladies, all in white with hoops and feathers, stood for hours with their chaperons waiting for a few brief, guttural, German-accented words from a little old lady with an irritable expression.

Jane suspected that her majesty found the affair quite as tiresome as she did. The two princesses in attendance upon her, a pair of dowdy middle-aged spinsters, appeared to be equally uninterested.

"La, but I am exhausted!" said Lady Hornby in the carriage on their way home. "I shall lie down until it is time to dress for dinner, and I advise you to do the same, Jane, so as to be in your best looks for your ball. Though your rank and fortune will bring you suitors aplenty, first impressions are all-important if you are to catch a husband quickly."

Surprised, she was about to deny any wish for an early marriage, but her mother leaned back in the corner and closed her eyes. Of course, Jane realized, the only way the marchioness could rid herself of the burden of her daughter's presence was to find her a husband.

Despite her plaint to Gracie that she was nearly at her last prayers, Jane had no intention of being rushed into a match she might later regret.

Nonetheless, she naturally wanted to look her best for her come-out ball. Arriving home, she went to take yet another peek at her ball gown, a slip of palest blue satin under a white net frock embroidered with flowers of cerulean blue. The tiny puff sleeves, low neckline, and hem were trimmed with rows of the finest Valenciennes lace. How could anyone fail to feel beautiful in such a heavenly creation?

If only Lord Wintringham were invited to see her glory! But no, far from falling in worship at her feet, he would doubtless stare down his haughty nose in contempt. She had deceived him, and she recalled uneasily his grim declaration that he could not abide deceit.

No matter, he was not going to see her. Three days later, taking her place beside her father in the receiving line, she anticipated nothing but enjoyment.

On her other side stood Miss Gracechurch, to be introduced to the Polite World as Lady Jane's companion, so that her subsequent chaperonage would raise fewer eyebrows. Jane was glad of her support as the *crème de la crème* of Society filed past.

"I shall never remember all their names!" she whispered in a brief lull. "I never dreamed so many would come."

"Between four and five hundred," Gracie told her, "according to his lordship's secretary, who had the unenviable task of sending out the invitations. I believe you will meet the same people wherever you go, so you will come to know who is who. The circles of the *Haut Ton* are of limited extent.''

Just how limited Jane discovered a moment later. Bobbing a curtsy to a plump matron in pomona green satin, she heard her father presenting her for the two- or three-hundredth time: ''Lady Chatterton, my daughter Jane.''

And after Lady Chatterton, their eyes goggling, came Miss Lavinia Chatterton and Lord Fitzgerald.

CHAPTER ELEVEN

DRIFTING UP through layers of sleep, Jane snuggled under the warm covers and mused on the joys of dancing till dawn. She had not sat out a single set, and whether the reason was her title, her large dowry, her new gown, or simply that it had been her ball, she had revelled in every moment.

Except . . . She sat bolt upright as the memory struck her. Oh Lord, Lavinia and Fitz!

Fitz had opened his mouth to say something that was bound to give her away. Quicker-witted, Lavinia had read the desperate plea in Jane's face and gripped her brother-in-law's wrist, silencing him.

"Please, I'll explain later!" Jane had hissed.

Lavinia had glanced around the crowded foyer and replied, her eyes sparkling with curiosity, "We shall call tomorrow, without fail, shall we not, Fitz?"

Fitz had nodded speechlessly, and Lavinia dragged him off in her mother's wake. Jane had exchanged a few words with each later in the evening, but they had both obligingly refrained from interrogating her.

Now she looked at the pretty porcelain clock on the mantel and gasped. Noon already! They might call at any time and if she was still abed the butler would deny her. She absolutely must speak to them today.

She rang the bell by her bed, then pulled the covers around her against the chilly March air. A few minutes later, Ella came in with a tray of hot chocolate.

"Awake already, my lady!" she said, her round face beaming as she set the tray on the dressing table and poured a cup. "I hear as you danced till daybreak. I could've got up to put you to bed."

"Gracie and I helped each other. Oh, it was such fun, Ella, even though Lord Fitzgerald and Miss Chatterton were there."

"Mercy me!"

"They did not give me away, but they are coming to-day for an explanation. I must get up at once."

"Nonsense, my lady. Here, you just sit quiet and drink your chocolate in peace, for Miss Chatterton won't be up and about so early after the ball."

"True." Jane relaxed against her pillows and sipped the warming drink. "In that case, I should like some toast and a coddled egg, and a slice of ham, as well."

"Makes you hungry, dancing, eh?" said Ella, and went out grinning.

While Jane was breaking her fast, Miss Gracechurch came to see her. She was fully dressed, in a morning gown of dove-grey merino.

"You are up very early, Gracie."

"Her ladyship sent for me," she said with a troubled look.

"What is wrong? She has not decided that you cannot be my chaperon, has she? I conducted myself with the greatest propriety last night, and I am sure you did, too. I will not let her dismiss you!"

To her relief, Gracie smiled. "No, nothing like that. In fact she congratulated me on my modest, ladylike bearing and confirmed that I am to be your companion. No, Jane, she wished to instruct me in which of your suitors are to be encouraged.''

"Suitors? After one dance apiece I cannot claim any gentleman as a suitor.''

"The marchioness is of the opinion that several of your partners may be easily persuaded to seek your hand.''

"Because of my fortune and because Papa is a marquis. I wish I were really plain Miss Brooke!''

"Come, my dear, in that case you would now be seeking a position instead of lying in bed drinking chocolate after your come-out ball,'' Miss Gracechurch pointed out tartly. "Believe me, you would not care for the experience. And believe me that you rate your own attractions too low. You are a very pretty girl, and charming when you remember not to be too outspoken.''

"Pretty?'' Jane shoved her tray aside, bounced out of bed, and sped to examine her face in the looking glass as if it might have changed overnight. "Am I really pretty? You have never said so before.''

"I did not want you to grow up to be like your... to be a vain, shallow creature to whom her appearance was the most important thing in life.''

"Thank you, Gracie. I should hate to be like...that.'' She shivered and hurried back to warmth of her bed. "Tell me what the marchioness said about my so-called suitors. Upon whom am I to exercise my powers of attraction?''

"Upon Lord Ryburgh and Lord Charles Newbury. An earl and the younger son of a duke, respectively, I understand.''

Jane frowned in thought. "Lord Ryburgh and Lord Charles. Oh, yes, I recall them. Why those two in par-

ticular, I wonder? Lord Charles is not much older than
I am, and he talked of nothing but hunting. Lord Ryburgh is not much younger than Papa and he waxed el-
oquent over his crops."

"Oh dear. Did you find them disagreeable?"

"No, they were as agreeable as any of my partners.
One uttered only flowery compliments and another
babbled of his winnings at cards. It is difficult to carry
on an intelligent conversation when one must constantly guard one's tongue."

And that was why she missed Lord Wintringham's
bracing company, she realized with a pang of regret. She
had had nothing to lose by speaking to him freely because from the first he had disapproved of her and considered her beneath his notice.

All the same, she did not want him to discover her
deceit. "Time to dress," she announced, once more
swinging her legs out of bed. "We must be ready to face
Lavinia and Fitz."

Miss Chatterton and Lord Fitzgerald arrived shortly
after Jane and Miss Gracechurch settled in the Chinese
salon set aside for their use. Unfortunately, Lord Charles
Newbury had reached the front door at the same moment. A solid young man, he eyed with alarm the spin-
dly false-bamboo furniture upholstered in delicate-
looking ivory brocade. He might be the son of a duke,
but his fresh complexion and his buckskins and riding
boots suggested that he was more at home on the hunting field than in a ladies' drawing-room.

Before he took his leave after a proper quarter hour,
they were joined by two more of Jane's dancing partners, followed by a matron with a debutante daughter to
whose ball Jane had been invited. For nearly two hours

a tide of visitors and polite chatter ebbed and flowed between the red silk-hung walls.

Throughout, Lavinia stayed stuck to her seat as if glued. Fitz, tiring of constantly rising to his feet to greet ladies, wandered about the room, pausing to exchange a word with an acquaintance or examine a black-lacquered cabinet adorned with gilt dragons.

At last Lady Bridges, Miss Bridges, and Miss Josephine Bridges took their leave. Fitz plumped down beside his sister-in-law, looked expectantly at Jane, and said, "Well?"

"Tea!" said Jane. "I vow I cannot speak another word without a cup of tea."

Fitz obligingly jumped up again and rang the bell. While servants came and went, Jane and Lavinia compared notes on which entertainments they expected to attend in the coming week. Lavinia promised that as soon as she reached home she would make quite sure that Jane was on her mother's guest list for her own ball, in a fortnight's time.

"I trust Lady Chatterton is not unwell?" said Miss Gracechurch, just as the butler shut the door behind him.

"Perfectly well, thank you, ma'am," said Lavinia. "She stayed at home to keep Daphne company."

"And the devil—beg pardon, the deuce of a time we had persuading her not to come with us!" Fitz exclaimed impatiently. "Now, Lady Jane, are you going to tell us what hocus-pocus you were up to at Wintringham Abbey?"

Pouring the tea into fragile Limoges cups, Jane explained about the carriage wreck, the decision to travel on the Mail, and the mischievous impulse that had led to her masquerade. Lavinia seemed a trifle shocked, but Fitz laughed so hard he had to put down his cup of tea.

"You had us all fooled." He wiped his eyes. "That'd make a dashed good story, but I daresay you won't want it noised abroad. I shan't tell anyone but Ned."

"Oh no!" Lavinia protested, wide-eyed. "Jane, it would be dreadful if *he* found out."

"Oh no!" Jane echoed with more force. "Not Lord Wintringham, of all people."

"No? Well, perhaps you're right. Ned's changed a lot since the old days."

Before Jane could enquire about "the old days," Miss Gracechurch asked, "Do you expect the earl to come up to London?"

"Yes, he'll be here next month. But he don't go to ton parties, and Wintringham House is in Grosvenor Square, about as far from St. James's as you can go and still be in the fashionable part of Town. You're not likely to bump into him by accident, never fear. We had best be off now, Lavinia, before my dear mama-in-law sends out a search party."

They took their leave, with promises to meet at Lady Bridges' ball.

"What did he mean by 'the old days'?" Jane wondered aloud.

"I cannot guess. Pray do not ask him, Jane; it is a personal matter and none of your affair."

"No, ma'am. But I wish I knew." She yearned to understand Lord Wintringham, to understand what had turned Fitz's friend of long ago into the unapproachable Lord Winter. Yet as long as he was in London she would go in dread of coming face to face with him by chance.

The butler interrupted her melancholy reflections with the delivery of a basket of grapes. Jane popped one into her mouth and read the accompanying card.

"From Lord Ryburgh's succession houses, with apologies for being prevented by a previous engagement from paying a courtesy call after the ball," she reported. "Oh Gracie, he is already wooing me with his crops! Try one, they are very sweet." Laughing, she held out the basket.

TOOLING HIS CURRICLE across Henley bridge, Edmund recalled how Jane Brooke had looked forward to seeing the pleasant little town with the Thames meandering through the wooded valley. And later, when Windsor Castle came into view, he thought of her again. Not that he needed reminding.

He had fought to put the impossible, impertinent minx out of his mind, without the least degree of success. That final, stolen kiss haunted him. How sweetly tender her lips had been, her skin like rose-petals—he groaned, a flickering flame stirring in his loins at the very memory of holding her close. For a moment she had yielded, clinging to him, a moment of rapture before she pulled away, sparks of righteous indignation flashing in her eyes.

She had threatened to swoon or scream or slap his face. Not for an instant had he doubted that the third would be her choice, but instead she had slain him with wit. In truth, he had behaved no better than young Reid.

Worse, for he was no ingenuous youth. He *must* see her to apologize.

That was the only conceivable reason for wanting to meet her. She had cut up his peace, insinuated herself within the walls that held the world at bay. She had forced him to see those walls as a defence, not the symbol of superiority he had thought them. Alfred had been inside the walls when Edmund built them; Fitz, absent during the building, had breached them by failing to notice them; but in twenty years Jane was the only other person to touch the man within. Miss Jane Brooke had observed the walls, and blithely ignored them.

He dared not let her come close again, yet he owed it to his honour to apologize. Until that was done he'd not be able to forget her. For just that purpose he was on his way to Town weeks earlier than he had planned, hoping that she had not already found a position and departed for some distant corner of the kingdom.

Not that he had much hope of finding her in the vast metropolis, he thought, driving through the Tyburn Turnpike then swinging right into Park Lane. His only chance was that the lawyer, Selwyn, might know where Miss Gracechurch was lodging. Fortunately, the fellow's first edition of Bacon made a reasonable excuse for calling on him.

Left into Upper Brook Street, and a moment later he pulled up in front of the classical symmetry of Wintringham House, facing south across Grosvenor Square. His groom jumped down and took the reins.

The front door opened as Edmund strode up the steps. His London butler, Mason, bowed and reported, "Mr. Alfred arrived with your lordship's luggage half an hour since, my lord."

"Very good." Edmund brightened, recalling that Alfred had intended to ask Miss Gracechurch's abigail for her direction. As he handed over his hat and gloves and permitted the waiting footman to relieve him of his driving coat, another possible way to track down Miss Brooke dawned on him: Lavinia Chatterton. She and

Jane had been thick as thieves. He'd be damned if he'd go anywhere near Lavinia, but Fitz could find out whether the girls were corresponding. Fitz, though no hardened gamester, was often to be found at the tables at White's in the early evening. "I shall dine at my club," he informed Mason.

"Yes, my lord." If the butler spared a thought for the roast turning on the spit, the pie crust browning in the oven, no reflection of it appeared on his wooden face. His master was to try him more highly.

"And I shall want a note carried to Bloomsbury in a few minutes."

"*Bloomsbury*, my lord?" Mason faltered. The Earl of Wintringham's frosty stare pierced to his bones. "Certainly, my lord; one of the underfootmen shall await your lordship's convenience."

Edmund found Alfred in his dressing-room, unpacking his clothes. "I shall dine at White's," he announced.

"Right, my lord. The fawn marcella waistcoat?" The valet grinned. "They'll be fit to be tied in the kitchen."

"In the kitchen? What the devil do you mean?"

"Well, it stands to reason. You don't come to Town that often, my lord, and they'll be wanting to impress you with extra-special grub your first night."

"They may impress me tomorrow night," said Edmund impatiently, "and I'll have something to say if the quality of the 'grub' deteriorates thereafter. You can have the evening off. I daresay you are eager to call on your sweetheart."

"My sweetheart?" said Alfred, startled.

"I distinctly recall your telling me that you were enamoured of Miss Gracechurch's abigail. Have you so soon forgot our stranded travellers?"

"No, my lord, but Miss Ella wouldn't give me her direction."

Edmund smiled at his disgruntled tone, though it meant he had lost one chance of finding Jane Brooke.

He walked to St. James's Street through the gas-lit streets of Mayfair, quiet at this hour between Society's afternoon and evening engagements. The dandies who sat all day in the bow window of White's, quizzing passers-by, had gone home to primp, but the card rooms were never unoccupied. As he passed through, in search of Fitz, a number of acquaintances greeted him. None asked him to join them.

He found Fitz at the faro table, a game involving a minimum of skill and a maximum of chance. A good deal of noise and laughter arose from the players, idle, sociable young men more interested at present in fellowship than the turn of the cards. Serious gambling for high stakes would become more general later, and continue until dawn.

"I'm off, fellows." Fitz pocketed a couple of guineas with an air of satisfaction. Standing up, he caught sight of Edmund and smiled a welcome. "Why, hullo, Ned."

Several of his companions looked up. Their boisterous jollity faded at the sight of the earl. Some nodded; others murmured politely, "Servant, my lord," or, "How do, Wintringham." Edmund nodded in response as Fitz came round the table to join him.

"You here already?" enquired Fitz superfluously. A sudden thought seemed to strike him and he went on in an apprehensive voice, "You ain't going to do the Season this year, are you? Her ladyship come with you?"

"My aunt is gone down to Kent, where my cousin Wrexham is involved in some sort of domestic crisis. Were she here, she would probably attempt to force

Lavinia or some other noble chit upon me, but in her absence I have no intention of doing the pretty to a swarm of bread-and-butter misses. I dine here tonight. Will you join me?"

"Sorry, old chap, I'm a family man now, remember. Daphne is expecting me. I'll take a glass with you before I go."

"How does Lady Fitzgerald go on?" Edmund asked as they made their way to the common-room.

"Blooming, though she won't be dashing about Town for a few weeks yet. I say, why don't you come and take pot luck?"

"Thank you, but are not the fair Lavinia and Lady Chatterton residing with you? Pray convey my respects to all three ladies." They sat down and he ordered a bottle of claret from the waiter who rushed up to them.

"You need not fear that Lavinia will resume the pursuit," said Fitz as the waiter departed. "Jane Brooke persuaded her she wouldn't like to be married to you."

"Has she been corresponding with Miss Brooke?" He tried to hide his eagerness.

"Corresponding?" Fitz gave a nervous start. Edmund realized his mama-in-law would doubtless disapprove of a friendship between her daughter and a penniless nobody. "No, that was at the Abbey, remember. They were thick as thieves."

Edmund swallowed his disappointment. "But as soon as Miss Brooke left the Abbey, Lavinia was in full cry again," he pointed out.

"Only because she's afraid of Lady Wintringham. She ain't afraid of her mama."

"I believe I shall keep my distance nonetheless."

Fitz refused to stay for more than one glass of wine, confessing with a happy laugh that he was a henpecked husband. After a delicious but solitary dinner, Edmund walked home, past houses blazing with light, carriages queuing before their doors and music wafting from within. He retired to his library—not so extensive as the Abbey's, but a good size for a town house—and took up a favourite book.

The printed words blurred before his eyes. One chance left. What would he do if Mr. Selwyn was unable to help him find Jane?

CHAPTER TWELVE

THURSDAY WAS Lady Hornby's At Home day, and Jane and Miss Gracechurch were expected to remove themselves from St. James's Place between the hours of eleven and three. Therefore, although the ladies had not yet left the house, the butler denied them when Lord Fitzgerald and Miss Chatterton rang the doorbell at ten minutes before the hour.

If he expected them to leave calling cards, in the normal way, he was sadly disillusioned.

"We *must* see Lady Jane!" insisted Miss Chatterton. "If she is really not at home, where did she go?"

Thus caught between a rock and a hard place, Arbuckle breathed a silent sigh of relief when Lady Jane's voice came from behind him, "Why, Lavinia, and Lord Fitzgerald. Miss Gracechurch will be down shortly and we are just going out, but do come in for a moment."

Jane, dressed in a modish pelisse of blue-and-green striped *gros de Naples,* led the way into the Chinese salon. Fitz shut the door firmly behind them.

"He is come!" said Lavinia dramatically, sinking onto a chair.

"Who is come?" Jane asked, though she had a disquieting feeling that she could guess.

"I told her there was no urgency," Fitz grumbled, "but she would have it you must know at once. I met Ned—Wintringham—at White's last night. You could have knocked me down with a feather. Well, I mean, he said he was coming up in April and it's still March."

"He is not..." Jane clasped her hands tightly before her "...he is not come for the Season?"

"No, no; no fear of that. I asked him outright."

"But White's, Jane! It is just around the corner, in St. James's Street. You might come face to face with him at any moment."

"I hardly think so, Lavinia dear," she said soothingly, though her heart pounded at the very thought. "After all, it is unthinkable for ladies to walk or drive in an open carriage in St. James's Street. On fine days we often go out through the garden directly into Green Park. I always carry a key to the door in the wall in case I want to come back that way."

As she spoke, the door opened and Miss Gracechurch came in. "Jane, it is time we... Oh, I beg your pardon, Miss Chatterton, my lord, I did not realize you were here."

"That's quite all right, ma'am," Fitz assured her, "We are on our way. I say, if you have no pressing engagements, won't you come back with us to see Daphne?"

"Yes, do," said Lavinia. "She would be beyond anything pleased."

Jane shook her head. "Much as I should like to visit Lady Fitzgerald and the baby, suppose *he* were to call on you!"

"Ned? Not a chance. He don't care to run the risk of meeting Lavinia," said Fitz with brutal frankness.

"Well, I'm sure he need not worry," his sister-in-law said indignantly. "You may tell him I would as lief not meet him either!"

Torn between disappointment and relief, Jane agreed that the Fitzgerald's house was probably safe, so thither they all repaired.

Daphne was delighted by Jane and Miss Grace-church's visit, and the baby cooed and gurgled and blew bubbles at them. They stayed for some time, before going about their errands. As Thomas followed them along Bond Street, from milliner to haberdasher to Hook-ham's Circulating Library, Jane kept a nervous watch for Lord Wintringham's tall figure. Twice she was startled by glimpses of the backs of broad-shouldered Corinthians heading for Gentleman Jackson's Boxing Saloon, but the earl did not appear.

Thomas was depositing the last armful of packages in the carriage when a cheery "View halloo!" announced that Lord Charles Newbury had spotted them.

"Care for an ice?" he asked. "M'sister says Gunter's is the place to treat a young lady, and Berkeley Square is just a step away, down Bruton Street."

Though bright, the day was chilly, but Jane liked the ingenuous young man and did not want to refuse him. He was so obviously pleased with himself for knowing about Gunter's. After consulting Gracie, she accepted the invitation and sent the carriage home.

Lord Charles hustled them along Bruton Street at a pace uncomfortable even for country-bred ladies. Arriving breathless at the famous confectioner's, they both chose a warming bowl of turtle soup rather than ices. Their host entertained them with a detailed description of a curricle race he had witnessed the previous day.

"Ashburton lost, so I'm out of pocket," he confessed, "but luckily Tuesday was Quarter Day so the dibs are in tune at present. I don't want you to think I'm a gambler, Lady Jane," he added anxiously. "I'd far rather drive in a race than bet on one. It's just there ain't much to do in London compared to the country.''

"You do not care for the city, sir?"

"Not I. Wouldn't come near the place if it wasn't for needing a rich..." Lord Charles turned scarlet and stammered, "Forget what I was going to say."

Amused, Jane took pity on him. "I enjoy the amusements of Town," she said, "though I like life in the country also."

"You do? I knew you was a right one!"

Miss Gracechurch said that it was time to leave, since Jane had an appointment to drive in Hyde Park with Lord Ryburgh. Lord Charles's face fell at the news but he offered to escort them back to St. James's Place, an offer that was gently but firmly refused.

As they strolled down Berkeley Street, Jane said gloomily, "Now I know why the marchioness wants me to marry him. He would carry me off to the country and she need never see me again. As would Lord Ryburgh, who is as obsessed with agriculture as Lord Charles is with sport."

"You do not care for the idea."

"I would not mind only coming to Town occasionally. In the country I can be myself instead of always acting the rôle Society expects of me. However, I have no desire to give Lord Charles my fortune or Lord Ryburgh his heir."

"Jane!"

"I beg your pardon, Gracie, but the only reason *he* has come to Town is to find a wife to provide an heir to his title and estates." She smiled wryly. "Especially the estates, and all that grows thereon."

"Have you met no one—eligible or ineligible by her ladyship's peculiar standards—whom you like well

enough to consider marrying?'' asked Miss Gracechurch as they reached Piccadilly.

Lord Wintringham's face flashed before her mind's
eye, to be instantly chased away. What nonsense! She
was not even sure that she liked him at all. She was saved
from having to find an answer by the need to watch for
a gap in the stream of stage coaches, barouches, phae-
tons, landaus, and drays.

A slow-moving carrier's cart allowed them to cross at
last. They entered Green Park and started around the
reservoir.

"No one," said Jane. "How can I consider marrying
any gentleman who only knows me as a prim and proper
milk-and-water miss? How shocked he would be after
the wedding when he discovered my true nature!'' She
giggled.

"I suppose you cannot be expected to keep up ap-
pearances for ever," said Gracie with a smile, then went
on hesitantly, "I was surprised, this morning, to find
you so adamantly set against meeting Lord Wintringham. I was under the impression that you were on
comfortable terms with him."

To her annoyance, Jane felt her cheeks grow hot. She
was glad of an excuse to turn away her face: to gaze at a
flock of graceful, white swans, with their bright, orange
beaks, that swam nearby.

She had not told Gracie about Lord Wintringham's
kiss, nor did she intend to do so. And that last evening
at the Abbey, she recalled, Gracie had been absorbed in
conversation with Mr. Selwyn when she and Lavinia sat
down to play duets and the earl stalked out wearing his
Winter face.

"Some of the time we were on comfortable terms,"
she said noncommittally, "and some of the time on most

*un*comfortable terms. I never quite knew what to expect of him. I wish I had not pretended to be plain Miss Brooke. He himself told me that he abhors deceit.''

"My dear, in those circumstances, surrounded by those companions, had you announced yourself as Lady Jane, daughter of the Marquis of Hornby, he would never have believed you. He would have thought you a bold liar, an adventuress, in short a deceiver.''

"So either way I could not win his regard.''

Gracie gave her a commiserating glance. "I fear not. I am sorry to learn that you wished to.''

"Oh, I do not care a fig for his opinion,'' Jane said airily. "Only, if he finds out who I really am, there will be a horrid scandal.''

"I cannot suppose Lord Wintringham to be given to gossiping!''

"No, but he has only to mention it to one person for the world to know. Where gossip is concerned, London Society is as bad as a country village, I vow.'' She sighed. "The worst of it is, I shall have to be even more on my best behaviour now, lest the tattlemongers find reason to gossip of Lady Jane Brooke. One mention of my name in My Lord Winter's presence and he will guess the whole.''

"It seems to me, my dear, that you care more for the earl's opinion than for all the rest of the world. You have painted in your mind an exaggerated picture of his importance, which I daresay a single meeting will cut down to size. Perhaps the impression he has made upon you is due to his being the first eligible and attractive gentleman you ever met.''

"Attractive! Not he!'' Jane denied with unnecessary vehemence.

They came to the green-painted gate in the brick wall of the Hornby mansion. Jane dug the key out of her reticule. As they walked up the garden between neat beds of crocus and daffodils and bare rose-bushes, an unexpected flash of homesickness surprised her. At home, though hills and hollows would still be blanketed with snow, green shoots would be poking through the soil in sheltered corners of the gardens of Hornby Castle. Winter was hard in the north, but how welcome was spring! Here in the city one rarely noticed the changing seasons.

Why had she been so eager for London when, in retrospect, life at Hornby had been so delightfully simple?

When they reached the house, Lord Ryburgh had just arrived. His ruddy, weathered face, the face of a farmer, broke into a smile on seeing Jane and he bowed awkwardly over her hand, unused to doing the pretty.

"If you don't mind, Lady Jane," he said, "instead of Hyde Park we'll drive out of London a little distance. I want to see how the winter wheat is doing hereabouts compared to Norfolk."

Jane met Gracie's eyes and a gurgle of laughter escaped her. "I had best change this pelisse for something warmer," she said hurriedly, and dashed upstairs to fetch her fur-lined cloak—and to warn Ella that Lord Wintringham had come to Town.

"I GOT YOUR NOTE, Miss Ella."

"I reckoned you must've, Mr. Alfred, seeing as you're here."

"How did you hear we was come to Town?"

"That's for me to know and you to wonder."

"Come here often, do you, to St. James's Park?"

"Aye, when I can. I like the band. Them soldiers play such pretty music."

"Not as pretty as you, Ella."

"Get along wi' you! Fair words butter no parsnips."

"I mean it, Ella, honest. I'd like fine to walk out with you. Where are you living now?"

"I can't tell you, Alfred, and that's God's truth."

"Why not? Your Miss Gracechurch wouldn't mind if I called, would she?"

"Give over asking questions, do. I can't, and that's that, and it'll do you no good scowling at me."

"Was I? I didn't mean to. Only it's a havey-cavey business, you not willing to say where you're lodging."

"I won't walk out wi' a fella as don't trust me."

"I trust you, promise I do. I'll meet you here, or anywheres you say. I'll meet you on top of Paul's steeple if you'll gi' me a kiss."

"What, wi' all them people watching! Oh, a' right, then. Just a quick un. Mmm. I wish I c'd tell you, Alfred, I really do."

EDMUND HAD TO WAIT three days before Mr. Selwyn was at leisure to entertain him. In the meantime, he went to see his own lawyer, Mr. Thorpe Senior of Thorpe, Morecambe, and Thorpe.

Among other business, he wanted to arrange an annuity for his cousin, Miss Neville, since she had left the protection of his household. It was his duty as head of the family, but he couldn't help thinking that Jane would undoubtedly approve. Old Mr. Thorpe, however, without demeaning himself by useless argument, made plain his disapproval, as he did of any change unlikely to earn him large fees.

Edmund's banker was more accommodating in the matter of a few minor changes in investments. Too many of his clients took no interest in the management of their financial assets, he confided, unless there was a drastic loss for which the bank could be blamed.

Duty drove Edmund to sit through an endless debate in the House of Lords on a minor change in the laws governing the East India Company. He had no interest in the question, but his vote might help garner support for his position on another subject when he did care about the outcome. For the same reason, he spent an afternoon at White's discussing politics.

The three days passed slowly. Early each morning, hours before the arrival of the fashionable promenaders, he rode in Hyde Park. He visited the booksellers of Paternoster Row and St. Paul's Churchyard, where he purchased several new works. By chance he came across Boswell's *Life of Johnson,* of no great value but he bought it on impulse. Jane might like to have it—if he was ever on such terms with her as to be able to give it to her.

If he ever saw her again.

At last Saturday evening came. Edmund dressed in his finest evening clothes, fit for a banquet at Carlton House, and then bethought him that such sartorial splendour might embarrass the lawyer. To Alfred's loudly expressed exasperation he changed into the less modish, more comfortable evening dress he generally wore in the country.

He was glad he had taken the trouble when he reached the narrow, cramped house in Hart Street. Mr. Selwyn's greeting was a trifle wary. They went into a tiny sitting-room and exchanged polite common places over an excellent sherry.

Holding his glass up to the light, Edmund decided the fine old wine was the exact colour of Jane's hair. He longed to ask after her, or at least after Miss Grace-church, but they were on terms too formal for any but the most casual enquiry. He had been foolish to hope that Selwyn might help him contact ladies who had chosen to conceal their direction.

After a few uncomfortable minutes the housekeeper announced dinner. The dining-room was not much larger than the sitting-room, able to seat eight at a pinch. The food was good, though plain. The wine, a bur-gundy rather than the more popular claret, was superb.

"Fine wines are one of my two indulgences," Selwyn confessed, "the other being books, as you are aware."

Once they began to talk of books, they quickly re-gained the easy fellowship of the days at Wintringham Abbey. After dinner they took their brandy, a richly mellow armagnac, across the passage to the library. As big as the sitting and dining-rooms combined, it clearly showed where the lawyer's priorities lay. Edmund ex-amined his Bacon and one or two other books of inter-est to the collector. He uttered all the right comments and expressions of admiration, but all the while he was wondering how to introduce the names of Miss Grace-church and Miss Brooke.

Chance saved him the trouble. "Shall we play a game of chess?" the lawyer suggested, indicating the board on a small table at Edmund's elbow.

"You appear to be in the middle of a game. I would not wish to interrupt it."

"The positions are engraved upon my memory. I can easily set it up again."

Edmund studied the board. "Are you playing black or white? Black? You have your opponent on the run, I believe."

"Miss Gracechurch is an exceptional woman," he said, his long face flushing unexpectedly, "but she has little time for chess at present. We play a few moves whenever she visits, which is more rarely than I could wish, since she is not often free and my afternoons are generally occupied in court or in my chambers."

Edmund scarcely heard the latter part of this speech. Rearranging the chessmen for a new game, with more care than the task warranted, he said casually, "So Miss Gracechurch is still in Town? And the young woman who was travelling with her... What was her name... Miss Brooke, was it not?"

"Miss Brooke is also in London," Selwyn said, his gaze shrewder than Edmund liked. "I have seen her twice or thrice."

"I...er...I expect I ought to pay my respects to Miss Gracechurch."

"You will understand, my lord, that I cannot divulge a lady's direction without her permission. However, if you wish I shall inform Miss Gracechurch that you consider it incumbent upon you to present your compliments... in person."

"Please do." Edmund suspected that the lawyer was amused; he was too gratified by the outcome to care. "Shall we play?"

Not until his carriage bore him homeward did his optimism fade. After all, why should Jane agree to receive him? She had been friendly, but no more so to him than to anyone else at the Abbey willing to respond to her overtures. That last evening, she had paid more attention to the others, chattering with Reid and playing music with Lavinia when she could have talked or played chess with her host.

At least she must be acquitted of any deference to his rank or wealth!

And then he had forced his attentions on her, his kiss no more welcome than young Reid's. Indeed, she had little cause to like or trust him.

Edmund reminded himself that the only reason he wanted to see Miss Jane Brooke was to apologize.

CHAPTER THIRTEEN

As Lord Wintringham entered, Jane curtsied. In Mr. Selwyn's small room his large presence was overpowering, and she was glad that nervous anticipation had kept her standing. Determined not to be intimidated, she raised her chin as if that would make her taller. She wished she had dared wear one of her new gowns instead of the far from modish green-sprigged muslin of Hornby vintage. Not that the most fashionable of morning dresses was likely to wipe the austere expression from his lordship's face.

What right had he to look so forbidding when he had agreed to—nay, requested!—this meeting? she fumed indignantly.

Miss Gracechurch, seated by the fire, smiled and nodded. "How do you do, my lord," she greeted him.

"Miss Gracechurch, Miss Brooke, your servant." He bowed, unsmiling.

Mr. Selwyn exchanged a dismayed glance with Miss Gracechurch and ventured an innocuous remark upon the weather. "The present alternation of sunshine and showers is said to be typical of April," he observed, "yet it is still March. I am always slightly surprised when Nature does not conform to our expectations."

Gracie said something about March winds, and Jane mischievously added a word on the subject of February fog. Whether My Lord Winter had anything to say of

January ice and snow she never discovered, for the housekeeper came in with the tea tray. Without asking, she set it before Miss Gracechurch.

A maid followed with a tray of cakes and biscuits, which she put down on a small table by the window. Jane took the cup of tea Gracie poured for her and moved over to the window, where she stood sipping, gazing out at the tiny fenced garden, bright with daffodils. This encounter with the earl was not going at all as she had imagined it, not that she ever knew what to expect of him.

He came to join her, standing on the other side of the table, and picked up one of the plates of biscuits. "Do you care to try a macaroon, ma'am?"

"Thank you, sir." She nibbled on the sweet confection of almonds and egg-whites while he went to offer the plate to the others.

Returning, he took a slice of seed cake and balanced it on his saucer. "Miss Brooke," he said stiffly in a low voice, "I have sought this opportunity to apologize for my unpardonable behaviour. Dare I hope to be forgiven?"

"Why, certainly, sir." She smiled at him, her heart dancing. "I shall gladly forgive you if you will only stop frowning at me as if I were the one seeking forgiveness."

His smile was uncertain but it warmed his grey eyes. "I beg your pardon, I did not mean to frown."

"Enough of pardons! Between friends they are unnecessary, and we are friends, are we not?" In a quake, she wondered if she had been too bold.

"I am honoured to be considered your friend," he said at once, to her relief. In fact, his response was sufficiently fervent to silence them both for a moment; then he said, "You have finished your tea, Miss Brooke. May I fetch you more?"

As he took her cup, his fingers brushed hers. Through her thin cotton glove—no kid for Miss Brooke—a spark leapt between them. To hide her confusion she reached for another macaroon, while he quickly turned away to ask Miss Gracechurch to refill the cup. When he brought it to her, they were careful not to touch.

The reminder of their kiss was too close, Jane thought. After another meeting or two, he would not fluster her so.

"Are you enjoying your stay in London?" he asked. "Have you seen all the sights?"

"A few," she said noncommittally. Between shopping and morning calls and evening engagements, she had seen little outside Mayfair and St. James's. "There is a great deal to see."

"If there is anywhere in particular you wish to go, I should be happy to escort you." He sounded oddly unsure of himself.

Jane racked her brains for an excursion that he would not despise, yet where she was unlikely to meet her fashionable acquaintances. "The British Museum?" she suggested.

"An excellent choice. You will find it interesting, I believe. Montague House is open to the public on Mondays, Wednesdays and Fridays, from ten o'clock until four, and I am entirely at your disposal."

Today was Wednesday. Would he think her too eager if she said Friday? Had she any afternoon engagements for Friday? If she had, she would cancel them. "Friday will suit me very well, sir."

This time there was nothing tentative about his smile. He really was excessively good-looking when he smiled.

"Friday it is. May I call for you in my carriage?"

"Thank you, but...but there is no need for you to go out of your way." Panic-stricken, she cast about for a reason to refuse his offer. "Mr. Selwyn mentioned that Montague House is just around the corner."

Though he looked disappointed, Lord Wintringham was too gentlemanly to argue. They arranged a time to meet at the museum.

"Will you have another macaroon?" he offered. "You appear to be fond of them."

"Tut, sir, a gentleman ought not to take note when a lady overindulges." She helped herself. "Especially since you have not eaten your cake."

He cast a glance over his shoulder at his host and said softly, "As a matter of fact, I abominate seed cake, whereas I should very much like a cup of tea. I have let mine grow cold. What shall I do?"

"Open the window, water the daffodils, and feed the birds," she advised in a conspiratorial undertone.

Grinning, he followed her advice while she made a loud comment about the beauty of the flowers, as if he were leaning out merely to admire them.

His cup replenished, he rejoined her. They spoke of spring flowers, and she told him of her feeling that the seasons passed unnoticed in the city. They agreed in preferring country life. Jane realized with chagrin that her mother would very likely approve the earl as a suitor, were he in search of a wife. Thank heaven he was not!

Through the open window came the sound of church clocks striking the hour. Miss Gracechurch rose to her feet, saying that it was time to leave. Lord Wintringham seemed about to offer to see them home, but Mr. Selwyn detained him with a question. The housekeeper showed them out and they hurried round the corner to Bury Lane, where a well-paid jarvey awaited them with his hackney carriage.

"How fortunate that Mr. Selwyn's sitting-room does not overlook the street!" said Jane as they set off. "Oh Gracie, I wish I did not have to pretend."

"Is it really necessary? You are not obliged to meet his lordship again."

"I made an appointment to visit the British Museum with him on Friday," she admitted guiltily. "Ella can go with me if you are otherwise occupied."

"Oh dear! No, I shall go with you. In that case, perhaps you had best simply tell the earl who you are."

"Not yet. Not until I know him better. Promise you will not tell, Gracie."

"I promise," said Miss Gracechurch, but she looked disturbed.

"WELL, NOW, Ella, we don't need to meet on street corners no more, now my lord's took up with your young lady."

"I'm sure I can't guess what you mean. Look at that bonnet, in the window there, the one wi' yellow feathers. Isn't that fine as fivepence?"

"You don't need no fancy bonnet to be the prettiest lass I ever seen."

"Ooh, Alfred, you do say the nicest things."

"I'll say 'em more often if you'll let me come calling."

"It's not that I don't want you coming round, it's just I can't tell you where."

"His lordship'll tell me."

"That he won't!"

"Why not?"

"Acos he don't know and my ladies don't want him to know."

"They don't? Whyever not? He'd come and fetch 'em and save 'em a walk or sixpence for a hackney."

"Look, here's a pastry-cook. My, them pies smell good."

"I'll treat you. You want a pie? Or one o' them French apple tarts?"

"An apple tart'd be nice."

"Here you are, then. Mind it don't drip on your gown. Come on, Ella, what's so secret 'bout your lodgings? I don't care if you don't live in the best part o' Town.... What's the joke?"

"Nothing. But I can't tell you why it's secret or you'd know what the secret is."

"I see what it is, you don't trust me. Like you said to me, I won't walk out with someone as don't trust me."

"I do! I do trust you. Only it's not my secret."

"I wouldn't tell my lord."

"You mean it, Alfred?"

"Take my oath on it."

"A' right, then. Miss Brooke's not Miss Brooke, she's Lady Jane Brooke, and her pa's the Marquis of Hornby."

"That's a fine Banbury story!"

"It's true! Why would I make it up?"

"Why wouldn't she want his lordship to know?"

"Just listen and I'll tell you all about it."

JANE AND MISS GRACECHURCH turned into Great Russell Street, hurrying beneath their umbrellas. Under the shelter of the porch of the British Museum stood a gentleman. Though he had his blue-coated back to her, his glossy beaver on his head, Jane recognized Lord Wintringham at once.

Turning, he saw them and came down the steps towards them, despite the drizzle. His smile brightened the damp, grey day.

"I hope we have not kept you waiting, sir."

"Not at all, Miss Brooke. I have spent an hour or two in the reading-room, and I just now stepped out for a breath of air. Good day, Miss Gracechurch. Come in out of the rain."

He offered each lady an arm and they went in.

As they wandered through the exhibit-crowded rooms of the old mansion, Jane was pleased to find that her reading had been extensive enough to allow her to ask intelligent questions. The earl had most of the answers, whether they were studying old coins, classical marbles, Egyptian antiquities, or collections of natural history and curiosities.

His first love, however, was plainly the medieval manuscripts. Jane wholeheartedly admired the jewel-like colours and gold leaf of the illustrations and illuminated letters.

"But I wish I could read the text," she exclaimed. "They all seem to be in Latin or Old French."

"I can manage the Latin, with a struggle, but the Old French is beyond me," Lord Wintringham admitted. "Come over here and see Chaucer's *Canterbury Tales*. You will like the portrait of the author standing within the initial *W*. Look: 'When that April with his showers sweet . . . ,' in modern parlance."

"Oh yes, it is delightful. And I can read the first few lines, but only because I know them by heart. I am glad the printing press was invented!"

He laughed. "So must we all be. Books were rare and precious when they had to be copied by hand."

"And still rarer when carved in stone," said Miss Gracechurch. "If you have no objection, I should like to look again at the Rosetta stone. Mr. Selwyn is acquainted with Dr. Thomas Young, who is attempting to decipher the Egyptian hieroglyphs with the aid of the Greek and demotic inscriptions on it."

They went back to the Egyptian collection, presented to the museum by King George after the British took it from the French at Alexandria. The Rosetta stone, a slab of black basalt, looked to Jane just like a large tombstone. While the earl and Gracie discussed the importance of being able to read Ancient Egyptian, she wandered off to examine painted sarcophagi and statues of gods and pharaohs.

Lord Wintringham found her poring over a magnificent collar of beaten gold set with turquoise and lapis lazuli.

"That would suit you," he said. "The lapis is the colour of your eyes. Beautiful."

His gaze was not on the necklace but her face. She felt the warmth rise in her cheeks.

In an effort to divert him, she pointed out, "It must have been excessively uncomfortable to wear so heavy a necklace in the heat of Egypt."

"True," he said, smiling, "and the lapis was wasted on them since their eyes were dark, not heavenly blue."

She was glad when Gracie rejoined them.

It was four o'clock and the museum was closing. Outside, the drizzle had become a downpour. As they paused beneath the porch, watching the raindrops splash in the puddles in the street, a carriage came round the corner and stopped before them.

Jane recognized the Wintringham crest on the door, having seen it at the Abbey.

"Ladies, I cannot permit you to walk home in this weather," said the earl with determination. "I am going to return to the reading-room, which is still open for members, but my coachman will take you wherever you wish to go."

Jane and Gracie exchanged a glance.

"We shall be happy to accept, sir," Gracie said composedly, before Jane had worked out an excuse for refusing.

"Good. Where shall I instruct him to take you, ma'am?"

"To Mr. Selwyn's house, in Hart Street, if you please. I must enquire of his housekeeper whether she has found a handkerchief I mislaid on Wednesday. Then Mr. Selwyn's boy will find us a hackney."

He acquiesced with a wry smile. "As you wish. Miss Brooke, I trust you have another outing to propose?"

Jane had a list, prepared in hopeful anticipation. "I should like to see the paintings at the Royal Academy, sir, at an early hour before the fashionable crowds arrive. Or Westminster Abbey, or..."

"Hold! Enough for the present. When may I have the pleasure of escorting you to the Royal Academy?"

A date chosen, he gave them each an arm down the rain-slicked steps, while his damp footman jumped down from the perch at the rear of the carriage to open the door. Lord Wintringham handed them in, spoke to the coachman, then stood in the rain watching them drive off, the brim of his hat dripping onto his broad shoulders.

Jane sat back with a sigh. "I was afraid for a moment that you were going to let the cat out of the bag."

"Jane!"

"I beg your pardon: to allow his lordship to discover who I am. You must admit that I have not used any expression of Derek's this age, and never in company. The museum was fascinating, was it not? And Lord Wintringham knew so much about everything. Can you imagine visiting it with Lord Charles, or Lord Ryburgh? Lord Ryburgh would be *aux anges* over the wheat harvest in the Egyptian paintings, and I daresay Lord Charles has never even heard of the British Museum."

THE NEXT AFTERNOON, when Lord Charles squired Jane to Lady Jersey's breakfast, she tested her assumption and found it true. Not only had he never heard of the British Museum, but the Royal Academy was no more successful at calling a spark of recognition to his eyes. Nonetheless, he bravely assured Jane that he'd be delighted to take her there. His relief when she declined was palpable.

"To tell the truth," he confided, "I don't care for art above half."

In view of Lord Ryburgh's venerable age, she forbore to tease him on the subject. She was surprised, however, to receive from him an invitation to attend a performance of *Macbeth* at Drury Lane Theatre. She nearly laughed aloud when he admitted, somewhat shamefaced, that he didn't care for the theatre above half.

"A fellow called Edmund Kean will be playing *Macbeth,*" he went on. "I hear he's all the rage, so I thought you might like to see him. I've borrowed a box from a friend. If you agree, I'll ask Lord Fitzgerald and

Miss Chatterton to join us. I know they are particular friends of yours."

Jane graciously accepted. *Macbeth* was one of her favourite plays. Besides, she had no intention of letting the marchioness guess that neither of the suitors she favoured met with her daughter's approval.

By the evening of the theatre party, Jane had already enjoyed visits to both the Royal Academy and Westminster Abbey with the Earl of Wintringham. His lordship had been charming. The two or three times some trifle made him poker up, she had succeeded in laughing him out of his haughty mien. As a change from intellectual pursuits, she had persuaded him to take her on the river in a steamboat one day the following week.

Fitz would undoubtedly have preferred a steamboat excursion to *Macbeth*. "I don't care for Shakespeare above half," he told Jane. "A good farce at the Haymarket's more like it, with plenty of singing and dancing. Trouble is, Daphne's taken a notion to see that actor fellow, Kean. She ain't felt up to going out this age and she wants me to go with her."

Lady Chatterton cried off with a megrim, so Fitz, Daphne, and Lavinia joined Jane, Miss Gracechurch, and Lord Ryburgh in his friend's box. The young ladies were seated in the front row, Jane in the middle. She had been to Drury Lane before and admired the magnificence of the theatre, rebuilt after the fire of 1809. Now she chatted with her friends and looked about the audience, nodding and smiling at acquaintances. All the ladies were fanning themselves, for the crowd drawn by Kean as Macbeth, together with the gas lighting, made the place hot as an oven.

The box next to theirs on the stageward side remained empty. Not until the house lights dimmed and the curtain rose did a gentleman enter it. He took his seat and leaned forward, his features clearly limned against the bright stage lights.

Jane recognized that profile at once: Lord Wintringham! She clutched Lavinia's arm.

"Are they not horrid?" Lavinia whispered as the three witches appeared amid thunder and lightning.

"Yes... No... Look, it's him!" Jane pointed and Lavinia gasped.

"My Lord Winter! What shall we do?"

"Wait. I must think." She had to escape before the lights went up at the end of the first act. Why had she not guessed that he was likely to attend the theatre? He was no wantwit, like some she could name, but a well-read gentleman of superior understanding.

Her mind raced, searching for an excuse to leave. The witches had vanished now, leaving the stage to King Duncan and his nobles, but the gruesome trio would soon reappear. That was her chance, any moment now.

The scene changed. *A blasted heath. Thunder. Enter the three witches.* A horrid sight indeed, withered crones with their hooked noses, beards, and missing teeth, laying their plot against some unfortunate sailor's wife. Quick, before Macbeth and Banquo made their entrance—

With a moan, Jane jumped up, knocking over her chair, and rushed out to the corridor. She leaned against the wall—on the far side of the door from Lord Wintringham's box—and drooped, trying to look as if she were about to faint.

Miss Gracechurch and Lord Ryburgh reached her at the same moment. Gracie looked suspicious, his lordship horrified.

"Jane, what is the matter?"

"My dear Lady Jane, pray take my arm. I had not thought...delicate sensibilities...I would not for the world..."

Jane raised her hand to her forehead. "Just a little faint," she said weakly. "The heat..." Her voice trailed off as the other three appeared, Lavinia whispering to her sister and Fitz.

Fitz nodded knowingly, his eyes quizzing Jane. "It's those devilish hags," he said. "Dashed if they didn't make me feel a bit queasy. Deuced queer fish, Shakespeare. You never can tell what he'll come up with next. Didn't I warn you, Daphne?"

A trifle bewildered, Daphne agreed, while Lavinia vigorously plied her fan at Jane's face.

"Nonsense," said Miss Gracechurch, her lips twitching, "it was nothing but the heat and insufficient nourishment. You must not blame yourself, Lord Ryburgh. Jane was foolish enough to allow her excitement at the prospect of seeing Kean in Macbeth to spoil her appetite at dinner. She will be better directly she has eaten."

Lord Ryburgh heaved a sigh of relief. "I ordered a supper at Grillon's Hotel," he said. "Daresay it won't be ready yet but they'll give us something."

He tenderly support Jane down the stairs. His and Fitz's carriages were sent for and they all repaired to Grillon's. Having dined well not two hours earlier, Jane failed to appreciate the meal hastily provided by the hotel's French chef. However, she thanked her suitor with earnest gratitude and apologized for spoiling his party.

"Not at all, not at all, my dear," he assured her. "Just as well we didn't wait to see Kean. I've heard his acting is overpowering. I never did care for the theatre above half."

After supper, he took Jane and Miss Gracechurch back to St. James's Place, promised to call in the morning to see how she did, and took his leave.

As Jane closed the door of her sitting-room behind her, Gracie dropped into a chair and demanded, "Well, now, what was that all about?"

"The earl—Lord Wintringham—in the next box. Oh, it was perfectly dreadful!" Jane clasped her hands, pacing up and down in her agitation. "How I wish I had told him who I am the first time we met in Town! He might have understood why I pretended at the Abbey. Now, after misleading him all this time, I do not dare to confess."

CHAPTER FOURTEEN

As EDMUND DESCENDED from his curricle at the White-hall Stairs, he wondered what had possessed him to agree to take Jane Brooke on the steamboat. It was hardly the most elegant of excursions.

He handed the reins to his groom and stood gazing at the Thames. A stiff breeze made the water's surface dance and sparkle in the morning sunshine. The river was dotted with barges and wherries, and the steamboat chugged upstream towards him from the Tower, a plume of smoke streaming backwards from its funnel. Definitely not an elegant way to travel!

Edmund wished he could have taken Jane to Drury Lane the other night. She would have enjoyed the well-staged drama, unlike the silly chit in the next box who had, he gathered, been frightened into fits by the Weird Sisters.

Turning to look back towards Whitehall, he dreaded witnessing her arrival in a hackney. He hated to see her in such shabby circumstances. But there she was, walking towards him with a youthful spring in her step and the cheerful smile that invariably raised his spirits. If she wearied of always wearing the same blue pelisse, she did not let it dampen *her* spirits. And why should she, indeed? Silks and satins could add nothing to the beauty of her face, her figure, or above all her character.

He went to meet her.

"I hope we are not late, sir? I would not miss this for the world."

"Your timing is perfect. The boat will be here in five minutes or so, at a guess. Miss Gracechurch is not with you?"

"Not today. She sent Ella, her maid, to look after me."

The girl bobbed a curtsy, her round face vaguely familiar; doubtless he had glimpsed her at the Abbey. As they strolled towards the steps, Miss Gracechurch's absence disturbed him. She had always accompanied Jane before, though of course she could not be expected to dance attendance on her young friend. It was kind of her to have spared so much time herself, and kinder to send her maid.

No, damn it, it was *odd* of her to spare her maid to chaperon a young woman who was no more to her than a friend.

Before he could follow through this thought, they reached the top of the stone steps down to the water. A number of people were waiting there. He noted with curled lip that they were all solid bourgeois citizens, most with wives and children, probably taking a day off from shops and counting houses to avoid the Sunday crowds.

The boat was close now, its paddle-wheels slowing. The shattering screech of a steam whistle momentarily drowned the regular thud of pistons. An eddy in the breeze brought the acrid smell of coal smoke to Edmund's nostrils.

"Is it not splendid?" Jane exclaimed in delight. "How pleased Mr. Ramsbottom would be with such evidence of British enterprise. I daresay he could explain how it works, too." She looked up hopefully at Edmund.

He shook his head with a rueful grin. "Not I. If you wish, I shall ask the engineer," he offered. Through her eyes he saw the steamboat as a bold invention, battling current and ebbing tide, gay with green and yellow paint and gleaming brass railings.

Edmund was not surprised when the group of people parted to allow his party to board first. Without considering the matter, he knew that his dress and his bearing bespoke what they would probably call Quality. He was aware that several of the men were regarding Jane with open admiration, while their wives eyed her unfashionable clothes askance. He ignored them; their opinion of her was unimportant, unlike that of the ton.

The boat drifted to a halt and a burly fellow, his bare forearms tattooed with snake-entwined anchors, set out a gangplank.

Edmund went first down the time-worn stair, glancing back often to see if Jane needed his assistance. She held her skirts up with one hand, displaying a neat pair of ankles. Despite this distraction he noticed that the last stone step above the gangplank was damp from the high tide. He avoided it, stepping across onto the boards, and half turned to warn Jane.

Too late. Her foot slid and she stumbled forward into his arms. He staggered backwards, clutching her to him. Somehow he managed to stay on the gangplank, but he would have landed flat on his back on the deck with her on top of him had not the big sailor caught and steadied him.

He let go of Jane. Breathlessly straightening her bonnet, she beamed with perfect impartiality upon him and upon the sailor.

"Thank you both so much for saving me. I'd have hated to land in the river. It does not appear to be particularly clean."

"That it ain't, miss," the man agreed with a rumbling laugh, "though 'tis a sight cleaner nor downstream. Watch out, miss!" he called to Ella, who was halfway down.

"Here's for your trouble," said Edmund stiffly, giving him a shilling.

He saluted with two fingers to his shallow-crowned hat. "Ta, guv, I'll drink the lady's health," and he winked at Jane.

Vexed, Edmund led the way to a bench he hoped might be sheltered from the smoke, if not from the breeze. Ella joined them, and Jane invited the maid to sit beside her. He fumed as they giggled together over her misstep. Jane seemed to have no notion of keeping a proper distance from menials—he recalled with a shock that she might yet become a governess, little better than a servant.

As if suddenly aware of his silence, she turned towards him. "Oh dear, you are angry. I am very sorry, sir, that I did not take more care on the steps. We could have come to grief, and how mortifying it would be to make a cake of oneself before all these people!"

"If I frown, Miss Brooke, it is not for that reason. I blame myself for not being quicker to warn you of the damp step."

"Then why are you on your high ropes—I mean, displeased?" She cocked her head enquiringly, looking ridiculously like a dog hoping for a kind word.

"I feel it is unwise to encourage such fellows." He gestured at the sailor, now making his way towards the engine-room as the paddles started turning again.

"Encourage? All I did was thank him and smile at him." Jane laughed. "I'd not call that encouraging him to do anything other than rescue clumsy passengers! But if he misunderstood, I rely upon you to protect me, my lord."

Disarmed, he smiled wryly and directed her attention to the arches of Westminster Bridge, looming ahead.

He enjoyed the rest of the voyage, despite the constant thump of the engine and the occasional whiffs of smoke as the boat followed the river's meanders. They disembarked at Richmond Bridge and strolled up the hill through the village, past the remains of the Tudor palace. As always, Jane was interested and appreciative. The view of the winding, islanded river and the woods and fields beyond delighted her.

They stopped at a pastry-cook's for a light luncheon, and then walked on to Richmond Park. Edmund told himself he should have guessed Jane would not be satisfied with a decorous promenade along the gravel paths. Instead, she set off across the rough, buttercup-bestrewn grass to get a closer look at the herd of fallow deer. He watched, amused, as she and Ella cooed over the skittish fawns.

They wandered on through burgeoning woods carpeted with bluebells. Ella's presence restrained Edmund from voicing a comparison of the flowers with Jane's eyes. Just as well, perhaps; everything to be said on the subject probably had been set down already by one poet or another, and he had no wish to appear trite.

The steamboat returned them to Whitehall Stairs beneath a stormy sunset that turned the river to a sheet of flame. Edmund's curricle was waiting, the matched blacks tossing their heads impatiently, but he knew better by now than to offer to take Jane home.

"I don't believe I have enjoyed a day so since I came to London," she assured him, her cheeks rosy from the fresh air and exercise. "We shall meet on Thursday at the Panorama, as we arranged?"

"I shall be there without fail." He bowed over her hand, then turned to his groom and took the reins as she and Ella walked away, chattering. If she turned south towards the slums of Westminster, he didn't want to see, though her comment about the nearness of the British Museum had suggested that she lived in Bloomsbury.

She must be ashamed of her lodging, wherever it was, or she would tell him where she lived. He couldn't bear to think of her in a mean tenement, surrounded by dingy buildings and narrow, squalid streets—she who loved the countryside. With luck she would find a position in the country.

She never talked about her search for employment. In fact, neither she nor Miss Gracechurch, nor even Mr. Selwyn, had ever mentioned her need to earn a living. He had only heard of it from Alfred, now he came to think of it, and that was pure speculation. Perhaps she was actually residing with relatives, which would almost be worse since she would then have no hope of leaving the city.

Yet she had never spoken of relatives, either. For all he knew, Miss Gracechurch was her only connection in the world, and she was not related.

A dreadful suspicion struck him. His shock communicated to his cattle and the curricle raced up Haymarket. Fortunately the theatre crowds were not yet about, but Edmund heard his groom draw a swift breath of alarm as they careened around the corner into Piccadilly.

He succeeded in calming his horses, but not his thoughts. Suppose that Jane and Miss Gracechurch actually were related? The only blood relationship that could not be freely acknowledged was that between an unmarried mother and her illegitimate child.

It would explain so much: why so refined and personable a lady as Miss Gracechurch was unmarried; why she was so solicitous of Jane's welfare. Their features were not alike, but their hair was the same shade and they were both above middle height, with slender figures. He was shaken by a sudden longing to gather Jane's slenderness into his arms. That ridiculous episode boarding the boat had been all too brief—not that his mind had been on the pleasure of embracing her at the time!

If it were true that she was Miss Gracechurch's natural daughter, he would swear she knew nothing of it. She was far too open and unaffected not to show it somehow. He must not let his surmise alter in any way his conduct towards either.

After all, he was only guessing, with no more foundation than Alfred had for saying she was to be a governess. He vowed to put the conjecture out of his mind.

Reaching Wintringham House, he went upstairs to change.

"Have a good time, did you, my lord?" Alfred asked.

"Very pleasant. Richmond is a pretty place, and the weather could not have been better."

The valet grinned. "Just like the company, eh?"

"Pretty, very pleasant, could not have been better—yes, that would not be inaccurate."

As he washed off the grime from the steamboat's funnel, Edmund thought of Jane's friendliness with the maid, Ella. He had disapproved of such familiarity with a servant, yet his own banter with his valet was no different. Of course, he had known Alfred all his life whereas, to Jane, Ella was no more than a friend's abigail.

Unless Jane was Miss Gracechurch's daughter....

THE VISIT to the Spring Gardens Panorama, presently showing a 360-degree view of the Battle of Waterloo, was followed by an expedition to Bullock's Museum in the Egyptian Hall. Jane continued as cheerful and amiable as ever, so Edmund assumed he had succeeded in hiding his doubts about her birth.

His doubts about the next outing she proposed must have been obvious, however.

"I know the circus is childish," she said, with the gurgle of laughter he loved to hear, "but it sounded such fun when Mr. Reid described it. If Astley's Amphitheatre is beneath your dignity, my lord, Mr. Selwyn has promised to treat Miss Gracechurch and me."

If a sober lawyer was willing to stoop to such absurd nonsense, the Earl of Wintringham was not going to prove himself a pompous prig by refusing.

He was prepared to enjoy the occasion simply because Jane was there, and to be entertained by her reactions to the show. In the event, he found much to admire in the horsemanship of the equestrians, despite their spangled tights. The jugglers, acrobats, contortionists, tumblers, and tightrope dancers were all the best of their kind, capable of amazing feats. And when Edmund heard Mr. Selwyn's guffaws at the antics of clowns and pantaloons, he stopped trying to maintain a well-bred reticence and laughed as loud as anyone.

That Jane forgot to let go his arm—after clutching it during the spectacularly dangerous trick of an equestrienne clad in little but a silver frill—in no way hindered his appreciation.

On his return home, after drinking a nightcap with Mr. Selwyn, he was met by Mason with the news that Lady Wintringham had arrived in Town.

"Her ladyship retired a short while ago, my lord," the butler reported, his dispassionate gaze fixed upon some invisible spot beyond his master's right ear. "Her ladyship expressed a desire to meet with your lordship tomorrow to discuss a matter of importance. Eleven was the hour suggested, my lord."

"Her ladyship's wish is my command," said Edmund with a savage sarcasm that made the impassive butler blink. He went up to his chamber, where Alfred was warming his nightshirt before the fire. "My aunt is come," he groaned.

"Don't I know it, my lord," said Alfred gloomily, helping him out of his close-fitting coat.

"She has summoned me to an interview tomorrow morning. I don't suppose you have discovered what she wishes to speak to me about?" He ripped off his neckcloth and dropped it on the dressing table.

"No, my lord, but it's bound to be nasty."

"You don't need to tell *me*."

"One thing's for sure, with her ladyship peering over your shoulder, you won't be popping off to places like Astley's no more."

AFTER HIS early morning gallop in Hyde Park, under threatening clouds, Edmund returned home to toy with his breakfast. It was ridiculous for a grown man to dread an interview with his aunt, but Lady Wintringham had the power to make him feel he was once again a small boy arriving at the Abbey for the first time.

He went to the library to write letters. Intent on making sure his instructions to the bailiff of his Staffordshire estate were easily understood, for a time he forgot his apprehension. Then the long-case clock struck eleven and a knocking on the door preceded Mason's appearance.

"Her ladyship is in the drawing-room," he announced, with a hint of apology in his manner.

Completing his sentence, Edmund dried the ink with blotting paper, wiped the nib of his pen, and reluctantly made his way to the drawing-room.

"Good morning, ma'am."

Lady Wintringham sat near the fire, clad as always in grey silk, her back straight and stiff as a poker. She raised her lorgnette and examined him from head to toe. "Good morning, Wintringham. You are dressed for riding." Somehow she managed to look down her nose at him even when she was seated and he stood.

And as always she put him in the wrong. "I beg your pardon for appearing in your drawing-room in this dress. I went riding earlier and I may ride out again, so I did not change. What is it that you wished to see me about?"

"Lady Chatterton informs me that you have not called upon her daughter since coming to Town."

"I do not care for meaningless social engagements and I have no intention of offering for Miss Chatterton."

"As you will." The countess sniffed. "The girl is not a particularly desirable match, but I had thought that her connection with your friend, Lord Fitzgerald, might predispose you in her favour. However, that does not alter the fact that your duty is to marry and provide an heir to the title."

"I am perfectly content to let my brother and his sons succeed to the title."

"Out of the question. To permit a collateral branch of the family to inherit *yet again* is impossible. No, you must marry, and if you choose not to select your own bride, I shall see to the matter."

"Thank you, ma'am, I believe I am capable of making my own choice," he assured her, striving to display as little emotion as she did.

"In order to do so, you must take part in those social engagements you shun."

"Surely not!"

"How else do you propose to meet a variety of suitable females? I suppose I could invite a number of eligible young ladies to the Abbey."

"Heaven forbid." Edmund realized he was outflanked. Still, he could concede on one point without losing the battle. At the least he would gain some breathing space. "If I must attend routs and soirées, then I must."

"Just so." Her ladyship's thin lips curled in a sour smile of triumph. "I am certain that you have been invited to the Daventrys' ball this evening."

"I have already sent my regrets."

She brushed away his objection. "No hostess will take exception to the presence of so eligible a gentleman. Despite your unfortunate antecedents, you are a splendid parti."

"This evening I mean to work on my speech for the House of Lords, and to write some letters."

"Letters!" Again she raised her lorgnette and peered at him as if he belonged to some distasteful species of insect. "Noblemen do not write their own letters; they employ secretaries. I advise you to do so at once. You

shall escort me to the Daventrys' ball tonight. If your
cousin Amelia were not expecting me at Danforth Place,
I should stay in London to ensure that you make an effort to find a wife. As it is, I warn you, Wintringham,
that if the Season ends without a betrothal, I shall
choose a girl myself and I shall make such representa-
tions on your behalf that you are honour-bound to offer marriage.''

Lady Wintringham never made a threat she did not
have the means to carry out. Recognizing defeat, Edmund bowed and stalked from the drawing-room. He
returned to the library to pace the floor.

He loathed balls and routs and breakfasts, where the
frivolous gathered to chatter inanities and the spiteful to
exchange scandal. Worse was the prospect of not merely
attending such assemblies but having to do the pretty to
coy misses, vain beauties, and haughty heiresses. Worst
of all was the thought of being tied for life to some
ghastly chit like Lavinia Chatterton or some cold, proud
female like his cousins.

The only person he could imagine happily spending
the rest of his life with was Miss Jane Brooke. Yet it was
unthinkable for the Earl of Wintringham to wed a
bastard—especially as he'd never be sure that she had
not married him for his wealth and rank.

CHAPTER FIFTEEN

"So what's that urgent you had to call me out to the pastry-cook's in the rain, Alfie?"

"Her ladyship's come to Town—Lady Wintringham, that is. You want a cup of chocolate, love?"

"That'd be nice. It's turned right chilly all of a sudden. Lady Wintringham's here? Oh lor, she'll be going to parties and she'll see my lady!"

"Not likely. She's not staying long and she don't go to nobby parties."

"Whyever not?"

"It don't suit her conseekence to rub shoulders with them as has more conseekence nor she does, and there's too many as remembers her pa was just a baronet. Likes to be a big fish in a small pond, she does. Leastways, that's what Miss Neville used to tell our housekeeper at the Abbey. Thick as thieves, they was."

"Aye, I mind Miss Neville. The little plump body, weren't she? But if her ladyship's not like to meet my Lady Jane, why'd you have to bring me out in the rain?"

"If I was to say it was just to see you, Ellie, would you be cross?"

"You're a cheeky one, and no mistake!"

"Well, it ain't *just* that, though I did want to see you, o'course. No, the trouble is, she's making my lord go to them parties."

"Get on! He's a grown man, she can't make him do owt he don't want to."

"The ol' witch has her ways. A right Tartar she is when she's crossed."

"You mean he'll be going to balls and that?"

"This very evening, he's off to the Daventrys' ball, and her too."

"So's my lady! Oh, Alfie, what'll we do?"

"SHOPPING is such a bore," said Jane as the carriage splashed through a puddle and turned into St. James's Place. "We have been at it all afternoon and I have nothing to show for it but a shawl."

Gracie raised her eyebrows. "I seem to remember that not two months since you considered the London shops one of the wonders of the world."

"Compared to Lancaster, they are! I enjoy having pretty, fashionable clothes, but I wish one was not obliged always to be dressed in something new and modish. Though I have two or three serviceable shawls, it will not do if Alicia Daventry recognizes one I have worn a half dozen times before."

"Miss Daventry is an agreeable girl."

"Yes, and she regards me as her bosom-friend, which is why we are invited to dinner before the ball. Yet she will not hesitate to mention to all the rest of her bosom-friends—quite in confidence!—that Lady Jane wore that old shawl again. So out we go on a wet afternoon to scurry about seeking a new one."

The carriage drew to a halt and Thomas escorted them to the door under a huge umbrella. As they went upstairs, Gracie said, smiling, "It is not only Miss Daventry's friendship to which we owe the dinner invitation, is it?"

Jane laughed. "Her brother has conceived a tendre for me, or for my fortune, but as he is the consummate Town Beau, the marchioness would never give her permission even if I cared for him, which I do not."

At the top of the stairs, Gracie turned towards her chamber. Jane was approaching her sitting-room when the door opened and Ella stuck her head out.

"Oh, my lady, such shocking news!"

"What is it? What has happened?" Jane asked in alarm.

Miss Gracechurch heard the exchange and joined them as Ella tugged her mistress into the room and closed the door firmly behind them.

"It's Lord Wintringham, my lady."

"Oh, what, pray tell me at once! Is he ill?"

"No, my lady, he's in the pink o' health, not but what it might be better if he weren't. This very night he's going to the Daventrys' ball."

Jane sank onto the nearest chair.

"How do you know, Ella?" asked Miss Gracechurch sharply.

The maid's rosy cheeks grew pinker and she hung her head. "You see, madam, p'raps I didn't ought, but the fact is I been walking out wi' Alfred, that's his lordship's vally de chamber. And...and I told him 'bout Lady Jane being Lord Hornby's daughter."

"Ella, how could you?" Jane cried in reproach.

"He won't never tell, my lady, honest. He's a good fella and he took his oath. And if you ask me," she continued with some spirit, "it's a good job I did let on or he wouldn't've told me about the ball."

"Gracie, we shall have to send our excuses."

"It is much too late, my dear. We ought to be dressing now. If it were only the ball...but we cannot upset

Lady Daventry's numbers at table by crying off at the last minute.''

"My Lord Winter's dining at home," Ella said.

"Then we shall go to dinner and make our excuses afterwards, before the dancing begins," Jane proposed.

"Unthinkable. To claim illness immediately after a meal is to cast disgraceful aspersions upon one's hostess's kitchens. I wish you will make up your mind to ending this hoax."

"I cannot, not now!" She shuddered, imagining the bitter contempt in Edmund's eyes when he found out. "I shall just have to avoid him all evening. At least Lady Daventry will not try to introduce him to me since she has hopes for her son. And thank heaven Lavinia and the Fitzgeralds will be there to warn me of his movements. But Gracie, if he sees you it will be almost as bad!"

"I shall seclude myself in a corner behind a potted palm with Mrs. Peabody."

"The old lady who has taken such a fancy to you? Yes, that will do, I daresay."

"'Tis all well and good, my lady, but that's not the end of it. His lordship's going to be at lots of parties from now on."

"How can he do this to me!" Jane moaned, hiding her face in her hands. "We must go back to Hornby."

"'Tis not so bad as it looks, my lady." Ella patted her shoulder. "Me and Alfred, we thought as how if he tells me which invites my lord accepts, soon as ever he decides, you can turn those uns down."

"An excellent notion," approved Miss Gracechurch. "I am going to change my dress now. Pray do likewise, Jane, or we shall be late."

Ella had set out a pretty ball gown of blue crape over white sarcenet, and a wreath of blue silk cornflowers and white daisies.

"Not that one," said Jane.

"'Tis the one you asked for, my lady."

"But I always wear blue when I am with him. He will recognize me at a glance. I know, the rose pink with the matching toque."

"But you didn't like the toque. You bought them roses for your head instead, 'member?"

"Yes, but it will hide my hair."

"And make you look a good ten years older, my lady," Ella objected.

"So much the better. The earl will not know me unless we come face to face. I wish I dared borrow the marchioness's rubies. Their magnificence would blind him, since he is used to seeing me shabby."

"Rubies! That you won't, or I'll be turned off wi'out a character. Her ladyship said as pearls is the only proper jewels for a young lady, and pearls is what you'll wear."

Trepidation destroyed Jane's usually healthy appetite and she did not enjoy her dinner. She was seated beside the Honourable Stephen Daventry, a fair, foppish gentleman in his middle twenties, who was not best pleased when she responded at random to all the latest on-dits. Nonetheless, he asked her to stand up with him for the first dance. She could think of no excuse to refuse.

The Fitzgeralds and Chattertons had not been invited to dine, but to Jane's relief they arrived early for the ball. As they left the receiving line, Lady Chatterton stopped to speak to another matron with a daughter in tow. Jane seized her chance and hurried her friends off to one of the small antechambers set aside for guests seeking privacy. Closing the door, she set her back against it to discourage unwanted company.

"Lord Wintringham is coming here tonight!"

"Ned? He can't be, Lady Jane. He's never been to a ball as long as I've known him and he didn't mentioned it when I saw him a couple of days past."

"The countess insists that he escort her. I had it from my maid who had it from his valet."

"Lady Wintringham?" groaned Lavinia. "Surely she has abandoned hope that he will offer for me! Mama has, thank heaven."

"What will you do, Jane?" asked Daphne anxiously. "Are you going to let him discover who you really are?"

"Not if I can help it. Please, will you all help me?"

"Of course," Fitz assured her. "Just tell us what you want us to do."

"Mostly to keep me informed of his whereabouts. Lavinia, pray stay by me whenever you can, since he avoids you, and Fitz, keep away for he is certain to wish to talk to you. Daphne, if you can bear to absent yourself from the festivities after so long a deprivation, perhaps you could claim to be tired and I shall accompany you to the ladies' withdrawing room. The less time I spend in the ballroom, the better."

"He will not recognize you from a distance in that quiz of a headdress," Lavinia told her candidly.

"That is why I put it on. It is amazingly horrid, is it not? Oh dear, I hear the music starting. Mr. Daventry will be looking for me."

"I'll go and see if the coast is clear," Fitz offered. He opened the door a few inches, sneaked round it and down the short passage, and peered round a pillar. From the rear, he looked every inch a conspirator.

After scanning the ballroom from his vantage point for a few moments, he beckoned and they joined him. "He's not here yet, unless he made straight for the card room, but he ain't no gamester. Being tall, he'll be easy to spot. There's young Daventry, Lady Jane, with a face like the end of a wet week."

"Can you see my partner, Fitz?" Lavinia asked as Jane slipped away through the crowd to find Mr. Daventry.

He was easily persuaded that she preferred to be in a set close to the musicians, at the far end of the room from the entrance. Edmund would not see her when he came in. The obvious corollary to this advantage was that she would not see him. Already the flower-bedecked ballroom with its glittering chandeliers was filled with glittering matrons, gentlemen in blue or black coats, and silk-flower bedecked damsels. The Daventrys' ball looked set to win the accolade of being described as a shocking squeeze.

Jane missed several steps in the more complex figures of the cotillion, in her effort to keep a watch on the entrance over the heads of several hundred guests. By the end of the dance, her fastidious partner appeared to be weighing in his mind the balance between her fortune and her clumsiness.

Fitz appeared at her side and murmured, "He's not here yet," so with tolerable composure she took to the floor again for a country dance with Lord Charles.

His lordship applied to the Dashing White Sergeant all the vigour of a country sportsman. Jane was hot and thirsty by the end. The silk toque had miraculously stayed in place but it made her head even hotter.

"Lemonade!" she panted, fanning herself.

"We'll never find a footman in this crush. Let's sneak into the supper-room."

She agreed; Edmund was unlikely to make for the supper-room as soon as he arrived.

Several other people had made their way to the supply of lemonade, champagne, and punch. Jane and Lord Charles stayed there, chatting to friends, until Lord Ryburgh sought her out for the next dance. Her hand on his arm, they returned to the ballroom.

As she stepped through the double doorway, in the centre of one long side of the room, Fitz once more materialized at her elbow.

"Ned's here!" he hissed.

She did not need the warning. Her gaze had automatically turned towards the entrance, visible now since sets were just beginning to form as the musicians tuned up. Edmund stood there with Lady Wintringham, Lady Daventry, and Alicia Daventry.

Jane thought him by far the handsomest man in the room, though his face was aloof, forbidding. Half of her wanted desperately to speed to his side and bring a warm smile to his grey eyes. The faint-hearted half imagined his aloofness turning to ice instead, when he realized that she had deceived him.

She spared a moment of pity for Alicia as she turned to Lord Ryburgh and said urgently, "I am still horridly hot. Shall we go out onto the terrace?" Gripping his arm, she tugged him towards the orchestra's end of the room.

"Is there a terrace?" he enquired.

"Of course, all proper ballrooms have terraces. Those tall windows on the other side open on to it, but we shall disturb people if we cross directly."

Though he followed her lead, he objected, "I expect it's raining."

"Surely a farmer is not afraid of a spot of rain!"

"No, but it would be unconscionable in me to expose you to a wetting, Lady Jane."

"Let us at least see if it has stopped." She pulled aside a heavy blue velvet curtain. "Here are the French doors."

Lord Ryburgh opened one and stepped out. "It is still raining."

Following him, she held out one hand palm up. "No more than the merest mizzle, and I believe that is stopping. I begin to think you do not want to be out here with me."

"My dear Lady Jane..." He hesitated as two couples came after them, the girls giggling.

She was afraid he was going to insist on returning to the ballroom. Turning up her face to the sky, she said firmly, "It is quite dry now, and the air is delightfully balmy. I do believe the moon is coming out. Let us stroll in the garden." She grasped his sleeve and pulled him down the steps to the flagstone path.

The damp, gusty air, scented with some flower she could not identify, was indeed balmy but not precisely warm on her bare shoulders. The moon emerged helpfully between high, racing clouds, to reveal a pretty little summer-house, glassed on three sides, that Alicia had once shown Jane. Thither Jane led her suitor. She was far too fearful of meeting Edmund to consider what Lord Ryburgh's emotions must be, until, seating herself on a well-cushioned bench, she found him on his knees before her. He clasped her hand.

"My dear Lady Jane, I had not hoped for such a sign of partiality, such encouragement I dare call it! I am all too aware that, though I feel myself in the prime of life, to you I must appear stricken in years."

"Oh no, my lord, pray do not..."

He took her agitated attempt to forestall a proposal as a polite denial of his venerable age. "Yes, yes, I am a good deal older than you, my dear Jane. You are too sensible not to be aware that I am therefore settled in life, not subject to the whims and crotchets of younger men. Certainly my sincere devotion to you is no whim. I believe we can deal comfortably together despite..."

"I beg you, sir, say no more." She pulled her hand from his, near to tears. "I am very sorry if I have misled you, but my feelings are not such as you would wish in a wife."

Agile despite his years, which after all probably numbered no more than forty, he rose to his feet and sat down beside her. "My dear child," he said with a sort of rueful sympathy, "there is no call for tears. If I have been misled it was by your mama's hints and my own wishes. Can you give me no hope that your sentiments may change?"

"I f-fear not, sir," she stammered past the lump in her throat.

"Then I trust we can remain friends."

His unexpected kindness was too much for her precarious composure. The tears escaped and, turning her face to his shoulder, she wept. His arm about her in a comforting embrace, he thrust a handkerchief into her hand.

"I w-wish you were my father," she muttered into the handkerchief, surprising him into a wry laugh.

"Perhaps it's a daughter I want more than a wife. Unfortunately it's a bit difficult to come by the one without the other."

That drew a watery giggle from her, followed by a shiver as a chilly gust of wind swirled through the summer house.

"Time to go in," said Lord Ryburgh firmly.

"I must wash my face. There is a side door we can use."

"Excellent. I must straighten my cravat."

She tucked her hand confidingly into the crook of his arm and they stepped out into the garden. Another gust whipped her skirts, and then, without further warning, a drenching squall enveloped them. Jane's thin silk was sodden within seconds.

Hand in hand they ran up the barely visible path, round the base of the terrace, and in through the side door. Her gown clung to her, her toque had collapsed in ruins about her ears, and icy streams trickled down her back, but Jane's only thought was that she had the perfect excuse to go home.

Lord Ryburgh promised to send a message to Miss Gracechurch, and Jane, her teeth chattering, hurried to the ladies' withdrawing room. There, happily for her reputation, she found three more young ladies who had been caught by the squall on the terrace.

Not that she cared a farthing for her reputation at that moment. Lord Ryburgh's proposal had made her quite sure that the only person she wanted to marry was Edmund Neville, Earl of Wintringham—but when he discovered her secret, her beloved Edmund would turn back into "My Lord Winter."

With any luck, Jane thought forlornly, she would take a chill and die.

CHAPTER SIXTEEN

EDMUND WOKE with a groan and glared at Albert through slitted eyes. "Go 'way," he growled. The sunshine pouring between the opened curtains started a steam-engine pounding in his head.

"Beg pardon, my lord, but you're expecting Mr. Selwyn at ten. Will I tell Mr. Mason to say you're not home?"

"Selwyn! No, anyone else, but I won't risk offending Selwyn." He began to sit up, then sank back with another groan, his eyes shut tight. The Daventrys' ball had been such a ghastly experience that he had overindulged in punch there and on his return home had retreated to the library with a bottle of brandy.

"Just drink this down, my lord," coaxed Albert. "You'll be right as a trivet in no time flat."

Venturing to part one pair of eyelids by a hairsbreadth, Edmund regarded the glass hovering above him. It contained a singularly revolting-looking, thick, brownish liquid, and the smell that wafted to his nostrils made his stomach heave. He hauled one leaden arm from the comforting warmth of the bedclothes and pinched his nose.

"What the devil is it?"

"A little remedy for what ails you."

"Where did you get it? I've never been top-heavy before in my life."

"I winkled the receipt out of Lord Danforth's man years ago," said Albert complacently. "You never know when something like this'll come in handy. Swears by it, he does. Drink it down quick and you won't hardly notice the taste, my lord."

Nothing could possibly make him feel worse, Edmund decided. He sat up and swallowed the stuff in two gulps.

For a moment it was touch and go whether he'd need the basin with which Albert had prudently armed himself. For another few minutes he was ready to accuse his faithful valet of murder. Then, miraculously, his head cleared.

Unfortunately, the removal of the steam-engine left space for memories of the previous night. His aunt had paraded him around the ballroom, presenting him to bashful misses and their hopeful mamas. Though he had protested to Lady Wintringham that his dancing skills, never superior, were decidedly rusty, he had been unable to avoid asking several young ladies to stand up with him. Faced with his taciturnity, not one of them had attempted any conversational openings.

Now, the next morning, it dawned on Edmund that what his aunt was looking for in the next Countess of Wintringham was not only birth and fortune but docility. The dowager had every intention of continuing to rule his household with an iron hand. The realization increased his determination to choose his own bride. He would seek out the liveliest girls, those with the spirit to resist her ladyship's domination.

Jane's voice seemed to echo in his ears: "I am not really a bluestocking." His own, answering: "Are you not? Pray don't tell my aunt. She will be sadly disillusioned." And Jane again, with a mischievous grin: "I would not disappoint her for the world."

"My lord," Albert interrupted the imaginary voices, "your hot water. It's half past nine."

He spent a pleasant couple of hours showing Selwyn some new acquisitions for his library and discussing his parliamentary speech with him. He had discovered that the lawyer brought new insights to the subjects that interested him. As he accompanied his departing guest into the front hall, he recalled his aunt's mention of a secretary. Doubtless she had some impoverished relative in mind, who would be properly grateful to her for her recommendation.

Rebelling, he said to Selwyn, "I'm thinking of hiring a secretary. I shall be glad of your suggestions if you know of anyone suitable."

"I'll give the matter my consideration," Selwyn promised, and took his leave.

When Edmund turned away from the front door, Mason was lying in wait. "Her ladyship requests a word with your lordship in the drawing-room," he announced. His manner held the merest touch of commiseration.

Edmund repaired to the drawing-room.

Lady Wintringham was seated at a small writing table in the window. Setting down her pen as he entered, she asked his opinion of his partners at the ball. She was most displeased to hear that he had formed no preference whatever for any of them.

"I trust you do not mean to be over fastidious," she snapped. "All the girls to whom I presented you are unexceptionable."

"And uninteresting."

"I daresay you cowed them into dullness with your proud demeanour."

"It was you who taught me, ma'am," he said coldly, "that the Earl of Wintringham is required to bear himself with pride."

She was momentarily taken aback, but rallied at once. "Of course, but a certain condescension is expected of a suitor. You are not the only eligible gentleman seeking a noble, well-dowered, conformable wife. Lady Chatterton informs me that you have already alienated Miss Chatterton and she will not force her daughter into marriage with a man she has taken in dislike."

"No doubt there are plenty of mothers who are less nice in their notions." Even as he spoke, Edmund knew he would never wed a girl who had been coerced into accepting his hand. He did not bother to tell his aunt.

She proceeded to give him directions as to how to make himself agreeable to a well-bred young lady. His mind wandered to Jane. He never had any difficulty making himself agreeable to her—but did she truly think him agreeable, or did she merely humour him because of his exalted station? Did she actually find their talk of books tedious? He heard her again: "I am not really a bluestocking." He frowned.

"Enough of that," said Lady Wintringham hastily. "You will know how to go on. By the by, Mason tells me that your visitor this morning is a lawyer, and that he has come to the house several times. You are not thinking of changing lawyers, I suppose. The earls of Wintringham have been satisfied with the services of Thorpe and Morecambe for generations."

"Selwyn is not my lawyer," said Edmund with a faint, sardonic smile, "he is my friend."

She stared at him, stunned. "Your friend! A lawyer cannot, in the nature of things, be friend to the Earl of Wintringham."

"He is an intelligent, cultivated man, knowledgeable about books, and I enjoy his company more than that of any of my so-called equals. I count his friendship an honour and a pleasure."

"Selwyn," she mused. "The name is familiar. I have it—was he not one of our unwanted guests at the Abbey? I knew no good could come of permitting such riff-raff to stay, and worse, to join the company. I suppose you are also on intimate terms with that encroaching midwife and the unspeakable cotton merchant. Ill-breeding will out."

Instead of his usual shame at her disparagement of his mother, Edmund found himself burning with anger. If he had learned nothing else from his acquaintance with the lawyer, the "encroaching midwife," and her proté-gée, he had learned that inferior birth was no indicator of inferior worth.

However, he did not dare mention Jane or Miss Gracechurch. They were within his aunt's reach and he had no wish to expose them to her malice. Selwyn and the cotton merchant could take care of themselves. "I have not seen Ramsbottom since he left the Abbey," he said evenly. "Doubtless he returned to Manchester long since. As for Selwyn, thank you for your suggestion. I shall most certainly offer him the family's business at once. Old Thorpe is far too set in his ways, and Young Thorpe has a shifty eye I do not care for."

Lady Wintringham's austere face turned an alarming shade of red as she mustered her resources for a blistering reproof. At that moment, Mason came in to announce that Lord Fitzgerald had called.

"I shall join him at once," said Edmund. "Is there anything else I can do for you, ma'am?"

"No doubt you will do as you please," she said icily. "I have made a list for you of the young ladies you danced with last night. A true gentleman calls to pay his respects the following day."

"Then I shall certainly do so, ma'am," he said, taking the list. He bowed and excused himself. Thank heaven she was leaving the following morning and would not return to London for at least a fortnight!

JANE TOOK NO ill from her wetting but, beset by blue devils, she willingly obeyed Gracie's order to keep to her apartment for the day. Donning a beruffled dressing gown of blue cambric, she reclined on the *chaise longue* in her sitting-room.

On a low table beside her stood a basket of apricots from Lord Ryburgh's succession houses, delivered that morning as a token of friendship, and the several volumes of Boswell's *Life of Johnson*. Edmund had described those, too, as a token of friendship when he gave them to her. How anxiously he had asked Gracie whether books were an acceptable gift from a gentleman to a lady, and then he had apologized that the set was nothing out of the ordinary, not a first edition. Jane had assured him, laughing, that she had not his obsession with first editions. The contents were more important to her than the date of publication.

As she found her place in the first volume, she decided that the giver and his recollection of her tastes were even more important than the contents. Yet she had fled him last night as though he were her enemy.

A horrid thought struck her. "Ella!" she called, and the abigail came through from the bedchamber. "Ella, did your young man say *why* Lord Wintringham has suddenly begun to attend parties?''

"It's the old countess, my lady, she's making him." Ella avoided her gaze. "Alfie says his lordship's got to find himself a wife or she'll pick one for him and that'd be a fate worse'n death."

"Thank you," said Jane faintly, staring unseeing at the page before her.

She should have guessed that Lady Wintringham had not given up when Edmund rejected Lavinia. He was being forced to seek a bride! So proud a man would never stoop to wed a nobody like Miss Jane Brooke, and when he discovered she was Lady Jane, his anger would far outweigh considerations of birth and fortune.

How could she bear to see him married to someone else? Even his friendship must inevitably be lost to her.

She sought forgetfulness in the book he had given her. Insensibly, Boswell's lively anecdotes drew her into the world of fifty years past. The sun peeked in at her west-facing window and soon flooded the room with golden afternoon light. The heartening notion crossed her mind that Edmund might go to balls just to mollify his aunt, as she allowed Ryburgh and Lord Charles to dance attendance upon her to keep her mother happy.

Recalling that tomorrow he was to take her to the Tower to see the wild beasts and the Crown Jewels, she resolved to enjoy his company while she might and let the future take care of itself. By the time Ella brought up a tea tray, with her favourite gingerbread "as Cook made special acos you're feeling poorly," Jane was restored to something approaching her usual cheerfulness.

Ella chaperoned her to the Tower next day. She and Edmund found as much entertainment in the maid's naive wonder as in the jewels and the animals themselves.

He did not mention the Daventrys' ball, nor his plans to attend others. Was he deliberately concealing his intention of marrying? Jane hoped he was simply too kind to emphasize the supposed gulf between them, to make her long for fashionable pleasures he thought forever denied to her.

As she dressed for Almack's that night, she wished she was about to have the pleasure of waltzing in his arms. At the same time it was a relief to know, via Alfred and Ella, that the earl absolutely drew the line at attending the Marriage Mart.

She knew also that he rode in Hyde Park early in the morning and avoided it at the hour of the fashionable promenade. Without qualms, therefore, she accepted Lord Charles's invitation to join the afternoon parade in his tilbury one sunny day early in May.

Lord Charles's superb matched bays were a trifle frisky, and when they reached the Park he decided to steer clear of the crowds in Rotten Row. At a brisk trot, they rolled along the carriage drive that curved towards Tyburn, past the Serpentine and the entrance to the Ring. They had nearly reached the Cumberland Gate when a curricle rounded the bend a hundred yards or so ahead.

Jane recognized it—or rather the blacks and their driver—at once: Lord Wintringham, with a young lady up beside him. She hastily lowered her frilly primrose muslin parasol in front of her face.

"The sun is so dreadfully bright," she exclaimed. "Pray let me down so that I may walk in the shade of the trees. Oh, quickly, please!"

Surprised and alarmed, Lord Charles halted his team. Not waiting for assistance, Jane jumped down and darted into the narrow belt of trees separating the Park from the turnpike. Her back resolutely turned to the carriage drive, she paused under an elm and listened. Surely Edmund would not stop to investigate the odd behaviour of a stranger.

Thudding hooves, the jingle of a bit, the crunch of wheels on gravel.

Then Lord Charles's aggrieved voice, approaching: "Deuced peculiar look My Lord Winter threw at me— like to freeze my vitals. Are you all right, ma'am? Quite a turn you gave me, dashing off like that, and the sun was behind us all along, not in your eyes."

"Was it?" Turning, she found him close behind her. "I beg your pardon, sir, of course you are right. I… The new foliage is so fresh and green, I had a sudden wish to stroll under the trees with you, who miss the country-side as much I do."

"Did you, by Jove!" he said, gratified, offering her his arm. She laid her hand on it and he set off at a long-legged stride between the tree trunks.

Jane was hard put to it to keep up without breaking into a run. "Pray go a little slower," she panted. "At such a pace we cannot talk."

"Sorry. You're such a Trojan, I almost forgot you're a female." As she blinked at this curious encomium, he stopped dead and turned to her. "No, that's not how it is. Can't forget something like that. You know, the marquis gave me permission to pay my addresses."

"The marquis? My father? When?"

"A week—a fortnight ago."

"He never told me," said Jane indignantly. "But then, I haven't seen him to do more than pass the time of day in at least that long. He probably forgot."

Lord Charles persisted. "So there it is, will you marry me? Do me the honour, my hand and heart, and all that rot. Hope you'll take it as said."

"No."

"What, you want the whole speech?" he asked in horror.

"No, I mean, thank you but I shan't marry you."

"Why not?"

"We mustn't keep your horses standing," she replied evasively.

"True, by Jove." He turned around and set off back the way they had come, at a comparatively reasonable speed. "Didn't I say you're a Trojan? Ain't many females would think of a fellow's cattle at such a moment. We'd go on swimmingly together, I wager. Come on, say you'll tie the knot?"

There was a small-boyish appeal about him that Jane usually found hard to resist, but this time she was adamant. "No, we shall not suit, I assure you."

"No? Oh well, you may be right. There's an heiress I've got my eye on," he continued buoyantly. "Her father's a Cit, but beggars can't be choosers. Pretty little thing, too, but she ain't got your elegance. Are you sure . . . ?"

"Quite sure," said Jane, trying not to laugh.

"AND NOW my lady's turned down that nice young gentleman, Lord Charles Newbury. Hark at the trumpets! Let's go sit where we can see 'em."

"Not too close, or we won't be able to talk. Look how the brass gleams in the sun. I bet them poor soldiers spend half their lives polishing. Would you have took Lord Charles, then, Ellie, if he'd asked you?''

"Like a shot I would. His pa's a duke, isn't he?''

"And if *I* asked you, Ellie love, would you take me?''

"Oh, Alfie, are you popping the question?''

"I am. I've growed that fond of you, girl, I've gone right off my feed. Well, will you?''

"I'd like fine to marry you, Alfie, honest I would, only how could I leave my lady? My mam was her nurse and Pa's her coachman, and me and Thomas has been wi' Lady Jane since we was old enough to go into service.''

"My lord'd take you on at the Abbey if I asked him, leastways till you was in the family way.''

"Ooh, Alfie, you are a one! But I don't know if I could stand to live at the Abbey, wi' all the upper servants stuck-up as their mistress. His lordship, too, for all he's come round a bit, I 'member how high and mighty he were when we turned up at the Abbey that day.''

"You can't blame him.''

"What d'you mean? Why not?''

"It's the way her ladyship taught him. I've knowed him since he were in short coats, Ellie. Master Ned, just five years old, and me not much older, and Mrs. Neville hired me to keep an eye on him. He were that friendly and that bold he'd toddle off to the farms or the village all on his ownsome to visit. Everybody were that glad to see him, from the blacksmith to Lord Fitzgerald, as was our neighbour. Master Ned and young Master Fitz was playmates. And then, what with one thing and another, Master Ned's heart were near to broke.''

"What happened, Alfie?''

"Come on, let's walk a bit, and I'll tell you.''

JANE NO LONGER took the air in Hyde Park. Invited to walk or drive with friends or a suitor, she would declare with a world-weary air that she much preferred Green Park or St. James's Park, less frequented by those with pretensions to gentility.

She no longer paid morning calls, except on the Fitzgeralds. One day Old Tom had driven her and Gracie up to Lady Bridges' house only to see Lord Wintringham knocking on the door. They hurriedly drove on. How dreadful if she had already been ensconced in the Bridges' drawing-room when he arrived! Ella's Alfred could not possibly provide notice of his master's unpredictable visits to the homes of eligible young ladies.

(What could Edmund possibly admire in two such fubsy-faced girls as Miss Bridges and Miss Josephine? Jane wondered.)

On the whole, Alfred's warning system worked very well. In two weeks, Jane only once caught an evening glimpse of the earl. As his valet predicted, he dined with the Frogmortons (Lady Anne Frogmorton was lamentably pretty, if one cared for brunettes), but he then unexpectedly accompanied them to the Dales' musicale. Jane, caught in a flurry of arriving guests, recognized the back of his dark head near the front of the audience.

She managed to step unobserved on her own hem and rip her skirt so thoroughly that no temporary repairs would suffice. Her escort, the elegant, dashing, and enamoured young Viscount Orme, was delighted when the mishap allowed him to escape the caterwauling of the latest fashionable opera diva.

He accompanied Jane and Miss Gracechurch back to St. James's Place, exacted a promise of a waltz at Almack's the next evening, and departed for his club.

"A rouleau unrouled," sighed Jane, sinking into a chair in her sitting-room and gazing regretfully at the torn blue satin. "This is one of my favourite gowns, alas."

"Perhaps Ella will be able to mend it," said Gracie. "The damage was no accident, though, was it?"

"No. I saw Lord Wintringham in the audience."

"As I suspected."

"How I hate going on like this, spending afternoons with Edmund and evenings avoiding him! Evenings being a demure young lady with people who expect propriety because they know who I am, and afternoons being my outspoken self with someone who does not know who I am. You may well laugh, Gracie, but I am so confused I shall do something shocking one of these days, quite by mistake. And don't tell me I should confess to Edmund—I dare not."

CHAPTER SEVENTEEN

SWORD DRAWN, shield at the ready, clad in a crested helmet and a short tunic, the Roman soldier stood just inside the entrance to Mrs. Salmon's Waxwork.

Ella stared. "Lor, his knees must've froze in winter," she observed.

Jane and Edmund exchanged a glance and burst into laughter. Silently Jane blessed Ella. Edmund had been sombre when he met them, and her own spirits too low to attempt to cheer him, hardly an auspicious start for an afternoon's entertainment.

"The Scots have the same problem," she said, gesturing at a Highlander in kilts, plaid, sporran, and bonnet, armed with a dirk and bagpipes.

"But at least they are accustomed to foul weather," Edmund pointed out. "The unfortunate Romans came from sunny Italy."

"They'd've done a sight better to stay home and mind their own business," said Ella sagely.

The first room was devoted to military figures, so they wandered on between knights in armour, Roundheads and Cavaliers, and amazingly lifelike soldiers of Wellington's and Napoleon's armies. By the door into the next room, the figure of an old man in the uniform of a Chelsea Pensioner was posed on a bench, leaning against the wall as if dozing.

Jane stopped and regarded it with approval. "An aged warrior enjoying his retirement after long years of battle."

The aged warrior opened watery blue eyes and sat up with a jerk, then clambered rheumatically to his feet, saluting. "Show you the sodgers, yer honour," he mumbled between toothless gums.

Edmund dismissed him. "Thank you, we have seen them."

"I knows 'em all, yer honour, like the back o' me 'and. Tell yer all the regimental 'istory, I can, all the battles, names o' the..."

"I said, we have seen them," the earl repeated frigidly. He took Jane's arm and urged her onward through the doorway.

She looked back and saw the pensioner's crestfallen face. When Edmund released her arm and turned aside to examine a Chinese mandarin, she found a shilling in her reticule. "Give this to the old man," she whispered to Ella.

Ella nodded and slipped away.

"This Chinaman reminds me of the chess set at the Abbey," said Edmund abruptly. He sounded self-conscious. "The one you particularly liked. Do you remember?"

"Yes, very well." She moved to join him, uncertain of his mood.

He looked down at her. "The old man's persistence annoyed me, but I ought not to have spoken so harshly to him."

"It was unnecessary," she agreed, surprised.

"You are good for me, Jane," he said with a rueful smile. "You gave him money, did you not? Allow me to repay you."

"What, so that you can take the credit for my charity?" she quizzed him. "Better to give him something yourself, as we leave. Look, there is an Indian rajah."

"He brings to mind your efforts to convince my aunt, by chattering of India, that you are a bluestocking."

"Ably aided and abetted by her nephew!"

He grinned. Harmony restored, they continued among waxen Africans, Red Indians, Aztecs, and Fijians, not to mention a number of rather more lively Londoners and country folk. Several apprentices on holiday had gathered round a display of a Turkish pasha and his scantily clad harem. Blushing at their ribald comments, Jane hurried Edmund past them.

The next room presented incidents from English history, beginning with Queen Boadicea and her daughters bearing down in their scythe-wheeled chariot on a terrified Roman.

"The poor fellow has cold knees," Edmund remarked, excusing him.

Laughing, Jane looked round for Ella. She must be still gaping at the world's strange peoples, for she had not followed them into the room.

They went on, past Harold with an arrow in his eye, Richard III smothering the princes in the Tower, Sir Walter Raleigh laying down his cloak for Queen Elizabeth to step on. Edmund paused to peer over Shakespeare's shoulder at the manuscript he was writing. Jane went on to look at the Gunpowder Plot.

The cape-swathed figures huddled around a pile of barrels were marvellously sinister, their grim, ruthless faces murderous beneath their broad-brimmed hats. Shuddering, she turned back to see if Edmund was coming.

Something brushed against her back. With a squeal she ran forward. By the time she realized it was not Guy Fawkes bent on mayhem but a small boy dodging past her, she was safely enfolded in Edmund's arms.

"I hope you will not suffer from nightmares after this!" His eyes laughed down at her.

Then mirth faded, to be replaced by a warm tenderness that quickly flamed into ardour. His arms tightened about her. Jane lost herself in his passionate gaze, feeling his need, her lips parting as he bent his head. Her pulse raced to keep time with the thunder of his heart against her breast. Instinctively her hand rose to caress...

"'Ere, this is a good un," sniggered a youthful voice.

"'Tain't zackly 'istorical, though, is it, mate," another chimed in. "'Is nibs's coat's cut by Weston if I'm not mistook."

Jane and Edmund sprang apart. Her cheeks burned. Glaring at the blameless Bard of Avon, she asked shakily, "Which play is he writing?"

The earl's response was none too steady: *"Much Ado About Nothing."*

She sneaked a peek at him. Like her he was staring at William Shakespeare and his cheeks were as fiery as hers felt. The corner of his mouth twitched, whether with anger or amusement she could not guess.

"Much Ado About Nothing!" She bit her lip but a slightly hysterical giggle escaped. "How...how very appropriate."

"Is it not? What was it that startled you so?" His colour was ebbing, his tone expressive of polite interest.

Jane admired his self-control and endeavoured to match it as she explained her momentary fright. To her relief, the jeering apprentices had discreetly disappeared. She showed Edmund the malignant plotters, who looked harmlessly inanimate now that he was at her side.

As they walked on through the next two centuries, Jane found Edmund's courteous but constrained manner more difficult to deal with than the occasional arrogance she was accustomed to. She felt herself turning into the demure, conventional young lady she despised. When they stopped before a splendid scene of the Battle of Trafalgar, she searched for a comment to lighten the atmosphere. Nothing came to mind.

They turned to the last tableau, the marriage of Princess Charlotte to Prince Leopold. A couple in the dress of prosperous yeoman farmers were there before them. They were not, however, admiring the plump princess's elaborate gown. They stared in puzzlement at a young woman in a plain grey dress and lace-edged white cap, seated on a bench close to the bride. In her hand she held a tatting shuttle from which depended a strip of lace.

"What's this un s'posed to be?" grunted the farmer.

Ella! She held herself perfectly still, even her breathing imperceptible. Jane touched Edmund's arm and pointed. The movement caught Ella's eye. She couldn't repress a broad, jaunty smile.

The farmer's wife jumped back with a squeak. Jane chuckled, Edmund grinned, and Ella bent double with laughter. Embarrassed, the couple hurried off.

"Them's not the first as took me for a waxwork," Ella gasped, rising to bob a curtsy. "I lost sight o' you, Miss Jane, so I just sat me down to wait."

"How consoling to know that I am not the only one so easily gulled!" said Jane. "I have been thinking myself the veriest widgeon."

"You cannot be both gull and widgeon," teased Edmund, formality forgotten.

"If I must be a bird, I should choose to be a swan."

"I picture you rather as a pert, friendly, cheerful robin, who brightens the dullest day." His voice was warm but he continued hurriedly, as if embarrassed by his flight of fancy, "Enough of birds. We have reached the end of the exhibition and Mr. Selwyn is expecting us for tea."

They strolled back towards the entrance, past the succession of historical costumes.

"This reminds me of the portrait gallery at Wintringham Abbey," Jane remarked. "Miss Neville showed it to me. I hope she is happy at her brother's house. Have you heard from her since she removed thither, sir?"

"Yes, and she sounds both busy and contented."

"I am glad. And what of your sister, Mrs. Parmenter?" The moment the words left her mouth, Jane could have bitten her tongue out. She and Edmund had vigorously disagreed about his treatment of Mrs. Parmenter. She had no wish to revive the argument, and her enquiry was ill-bred since, as he must guess, her interest was not in the lady's health but in her financial situation.

The damage was done. His brows drew together in a frown, his nostrils flared, and he said frostily, "I believe my sister is well."

Jane wanted to curl up and die. After his charming, heart-warming compliment comparing her to a robin, how could she have been so gauche as to make him withdraw again into the bleak vaults of family pride? Yet she had her own pride. She had never let him daunt her, and her realization that she loved him must not be allowed to make her timid.

"And Lady Wintringham?" she asked, as casually as she could manage.

"Well, as always." He looked down at her, his face grim but the unmistakable beginning of a twinkle in his eyes. "It is beneath my aunt's dignity to permit a mere illness to encroach upon her."

"Of course, I should have known." She smiled at him, while inside she uttered a silent crow of triumph. Bold defiance of his haughtiness was the only way to extricate him from that unhappy mood. To truckle to it, or to whine, as his sister had, merely reinforced his contempt.

She was gratified when, though his good humour was not entirely restored, he remembered to tip the Chelsea Pensioner on the way out.

It was raining heavily, and she was glad to be able to accept a ride in his carriage for once, since they were going to Mr. Selwyn's. His footman sheltering them with an umbrella, he handed her in, then Ella, then joined them.

As he sat down beside Jane, he spoke softly so as not to be heard by the maid on the opposite seat. "I have not heard from Judith since she left the Abbey, so I assume Parmenter has not been arrested for debt. I told you she was cozening me, did I not?"

She recalled all too well his harsh condemnation: "I cannot abide deceit." Her self-satisfaction fled.

Miss Gracechurch was already at Mr. Selwyn's when they arrived. Jane did not draw aside with Edmund, as had become their habit, but sat quietly next to her chaperon. She tried to listen to the conversation but those four words from the past haunted her. He had turned his coldness on her for simply asking about his sister. If—no, *when;* sooner or later the truth was bound to be discovered—*when* he learned of her deception, he would loathe her.

He would loathe her, though he had laughed with her, had called her a robin who brightened his day, had so nearly kissed her. That memory made her heart lurch and her whole body tingle. As if she feared he might read her mind, her gaze flew to his face, but he was answering some query of Mr. Selwyn's, not even looking her way.

She concentrated on his intelligence, his sense of humour, his willingness to credit her intelligence, his kindness—when he forgot his frigid arrogance. Edmund might forgive her imposture. My Lord Winter never would.

If only she were not Lady Jane, daughter of the Marquis of Hornby!

Yet that was no solution. Plain Miss Jane Brooke was his friend but could never aspire to a closer relationship. He was ashamed to be seen with her, or why did he never invite her...

"Jane, it is time we were going," said Gracie. "You are in a brown study this afternoon!"

She realized that Edmund was watching her with evident anxiety. When she took her leave of him, he said in a low voice, "You have been very quiet. Have I offended you, Miss Jane?"

"No, not at all." She made a feeble attempt at drollery. "I am a little tired after being frightened half out of my wits by Guy Fawkes."

Though he smiled, the concern in his eyes was unabated. "I must leave Town on Friday for a few days," he said. "There are one or two problems at my Dorset manor that I must deal with in person. I trust you will have recovered from your fright before I go. Let us make an appointment to visit Burford's Panorama on Thursday, unless you would prefer to investigate the booksellers of Paternoster Row?''

"Either will be delightful, sir," she murmured listlessly.

With a searching look, he bowed over her hand before turning to say goodbye to Miss Gracechurch.

Because of the rain, Mr. Selwyn had sent his boy to bring their waiting hackney to the door. Jane, Gracie, and Ella squeezed into the shabby vehicle and the bony nag clopped slowly down Hart Street.

"Burford's Panorama!" Jane pronounced with passionate resentment. "Paternoster Row! Why does he never invite me to the theatre, or to a concert, or to drive in Hyde Park, or even to Vauxhall Gardens? I could not accept, but he might at least offer! He is ashamed to be seen with me."

"My dear, his lordship is solicitous of your reputation."

"My reputation?"

"The earl is undoubtedly aware that any pretty young lady unknown to the ton—as he supposes you—yet seen with him in a public place must inevitably be taken for his *chère amie.*"

Jane had to admit that Gracie was probably right, but she was not ready to give up her grievance. "He could at least ask me to drive with him elsewhere."

"He has, I am glad to say, too much delicacy by far. For a gentleman to take a young lady up for a turn about the Park is perfectly proper. For Lord Wintringham to invite you to drive alone with him other than in one of the parks would suggest that he takes you for a light-skirt.''

"Oh." She sighed. "Then I must be happy that he does not. I daresay there is an equally valid reason why he cannot hold a dinner party in his own home and invite both of us to meet his friends?"

Gracie smiled wryly. "I doubt the reason will make you happy. To do so would amount to a declaration that he intends to ask for your hand, so if he does not..."

"It means he does not consider me worthy to be his bride. I wish I had not asked. Oh, I do not understand him! How can the same man be both my dear friend and My Lord Winter? I have suitors as nobly born as he who have not one half—one tenth!—his arrogance, and none of his cold hauteur."

" 'Tis all his aunt's fault, my lady," Ella volunteered.

"What?" Leaning forward, Jane stared at her abigail. "What do you know of it?"

"Alfie...Mr. Alfred told me all about his lordship. He were the cheerfullest, friendliest little boy you could hope to see. Then, all at once, when he were ten or eleven or thereabouts, first his ma died, then his cousin died that was son and heir to the old earl. So then his pa was heir, and young Master Ned after him. Both on 'em was that upset acos o' Mrs. Neville dying, and while they was all at sixes and sevens Lady Wintringham come along and says she's a-going to bring up Master Ned now, to teach him his duty."

"She took him away from his family at such a time?" asked Jane, shocked.

"That she did, my lady. She didn't approve o' Mr. Neville acos he married beneath him, Mrs. Neville being naught but a sea-captain's daughter. Her ladyship were too old to have another child, so she swore she'd make Master Ned fit to take her son's place. She took him off to that great, draughty Abbey, where his top-lofty cousins looked down on him. She taught him he weren't good enough to be Earl of Wintringham but he were too good to hob-nob wi' the rest o' the world. He were only a little boy, my lady, what could he do but believe her?''

"How unhappy he must have been!" Jane cried.

"Aye, that he were."

"Surely his father could have taken him home?"

"Now that's the worst of it, to my way of thinking. You see, Master Ned didn't want to go off wi' his aunt, o' course, but then Mr. Neville let him take Alfie wi' him and promised he could come home if he weren't happy. Well, Alfie stuck by him through thick and thin, whatever her ladyship tried, but his pa let him down. Alfie says he weren't never the same after his wife died, and he hadn't got the strength to fight Lady Wintringham. Only to Master Ned it just seemed like his pa never meant to keep his promise.''

Jane sank back against the shabby squabs and buried her face in her hands. "No wonder he abhors deceit!" she wailed despairingly.

CHAPTER EIGHTEEN

EDMUND GAZED around the ballroom. He found the glittering assembly much less attractive than that afternoon's waxen crowd. There was Lady Jersey, tearing someone's reputation to shreds with her sharp tongue; Lord Sefton, who had gambled away a fortune and recouped it by enclosing the land of his poorer neighbours; Lady Oxford, each of whose children was reputed to have a different father; Lord Hertford, a nonentity who owed his position as Lord Chancellor to his wife's position as Prinny's favourite.

There was golden-haired Lady Hornby, a dainty doll surrounded by admirers, but mutton dressed as lamb, since by all accounts she had a daughter old enough to make her come-out; rumour had it that the girl was not allowed to appear at the same functions as her mother lest the marchioness's true age be remarked upon.

And there, thank heaven, was Fitz, though unfortunately accompanied by his wife and sister-in-law. Edmund braced himself. Lavinia Chatterton was certainly no worse than the other young ladies who, for the past few weeks, had been induced by ambition or by ambitious mamas to pursue him. Indeed, Lavinia might even be better than most, for had not Jane befriended her at the Abbey?

He made his way around the room and greeted the Fitzgeralds, then turned to Lavinia, bowed and requested, "May I have the honour of the next dance, Miss

Chatterton?'' Noting her alarm, he added dryly, ''I promise not to propose marriage.''

She giggled. ''I am engaged for the next, my lord, but I have a country dance free later on, if you wish it. And it would do you no good to propose marriage, for I have an Understanding with Mr. Arthur Meade. He is gone into Lincolnshire to ask Papa's permission.''

''Lord Meade's heir? My felicitations, ma'am.'' He wrote his name on her card and went reluctantly in search of another partner. At least she had answered him honestly.

He could not say the same for any of the young ladies he subsequently stood up with. They all said what they thought he wanted to hear and they bored him. Worse, he knew they tried to please him not because they liked him but because he was a ''Catch.'' Behind his back they laughed at his stiff manners. Yet any of them would consider marriage with the Earl of Wintringham a feather in her cap, with lack of affection of no importance whatever.

Lavinia, her spine stiffened by her brief encounter with Jane, had the courage to follow her own inclination. Edmund began to look forward to his dance with her.

He was disappointed. She was uneasy when he led her onto the floor, and each time she opened her mouth to answer his polite queries about her enjoyment of the London Season, she paused as if to censor herself.

''You need not fear that I shall suddenly decide to seek your hand, you know,'' he said sarcastically as he took her back to her sister. ''Is that why you have been biting your tongue?''

''No...yes...no, my lord,'' she said, flustered. ''That is, if Mama hears that you stood up with me, her hopes may revive.''

"Then doubtless they will wither again when I do not call tomorrow."

Her relief was not flattering.

When they arrived, Fitz was bending solicitously over his wife. He straightened. "Lavinia, Daphne's tired. I'm going to take her home, but if you wish to stay I daresay we can find a lady to chaperon you and I'll come back to fetch you."

"Oh no, I shall go with you. The ball is monstrous dull with Arthur gone."

Edmund suddenly wondered if he might have enjoyed the tedious affair had Jane been there. She was not, and he could not bear to stand up with another hopeful, toad-eating partner. "I am leaving, too," he said abruptly.

"Come with us, Ned, and join me for a game of billiards and a nightcap," Fitz invited him.

When he hesitated, Lady Fitzgerald added her soft voice, saying she felt guilty because Fitz spent so much time dancing attendance on her that he scarcely saw his friends. So Edmund accepted. It was better than going home to brood on Jane's unwonted reticence and to ask himself for the hundredth time whether she guessed how nearly he had kissed her.

As soon as they reached the Fitzgeralds' house, the ladies retired. Edmund and Fitz repaired to the room the latter laughably called his library, which had earned that name with three shelves of novels and an outdated edition of Debrett's *Peerage*. Its chief feature was a billiard table. Fitz poured brandy from a decanter and they began a game.

Edmund wasn't concentrating. Playing a poor shot, he said enviously, "You're a lucky man."

"Because I generally beat you? Gammon, it's sheer skill."

"No, not that. If I'm not mistaken, you are in love with your wife, and she with you."

Fitz beamed. "Yes, damme if I ain't the luckiest man in the world."

"I have been haunting the ballrooms for weeks now, and I've not found a single eligible female I care a groat for." Chalking his cue, he sighed. "Nor, I confess, have I the trick of making myself agreeable."

"Oh, I don't know," Fitz consoled him. He leaned over the table, eyed the balls carefully, and with one stroke pocketed all three. "You haven't the knack of doing the pretty, but just make a try at fixing your interest and I daresay there's not a one wouldn't have you."

"That goes without saying. They are all heels over head in love with my purse and my title. It will have to be a marriage of convenience."

"Lady Wintringham's plaguing you, is she?"

"She will return to Town soon, and if I don't have a name or two to offer she'll..." Edmund stopped dead in the middle of a shot, set down his cue among the balls, straightened, and staring unseeingly at his friend said, "Fitz, I'm a fool."

"Well, I don't know that I'd go that far." Fitz delicately removed the cue from the table. "Though I must say that's a devilish odd thing to do in the middle of a game, even if you are losing."

"I'm an unmitigated fool, a jobbernowl, a knock in the cradle, any name you want to call me. But thank heaven I have seen the light in time." His heart sang. "If I'm to marry a woman who loves only my fortune and rank, why should I not at least marry a woman I love?"

"A woman you love?" said Fitz cautiously. "Didn't you just say you don't care a groat..."

"Do you recall Miss Brooke?"

"Miss Brooke?"

"Miss Jane Brooke. One of the fog-bound travellers at the Abbey. Surely you remember her! She helped deliver your child."

"Er, um, well, yes, as a matter of fact I do remember her. I, er, to tell the truth, she's come here to see Daphne and the baby. Just once or twice."

Edmund frowned. "She has? Neither of you has mentioned it to me! There is some mystery that I must... No, never mind." He had finally come to his senses. He didn't give a damn if Jane only wanted the security he could offer her. He didn't give a damn if she were baseborn. But let the world get a whiff of mystery and some scandalmonger was bound to ferret out the truth of her parentage. "I'm going to marry her," he said simply.

"Marry Ja...Miss Brooke?" Fitz's mouth dropped open. "Oh my God!"

"Why not? I never thought you were so high in the instep."

"No, no, I'm not, I assure you. I'm devilish fond of Ja...Miss Brooke, and so are Daphne and Lavinia. Not but what I did think you..." he added questioningly.

"I love her. What does her lack of rank, or anything else, matter? But listen, Fitz, not a word to a soul, not even Lavinia or your wife. Just let my aunt catch the slightest hint before the knot is tied and she will find a way to put a spoke in my wheel. I shall get a licence tomorrow. Jane and Miss Gracechurch will come to Dorset with me on Friday and we'll do the thing there. My aunt shall be presented with a *fait accompli.*"

"Er, I don't want to be a wet blanket, old chap, but can you be sure Miss Brooke will accept?"

"You yourself said that any of the most eligible young ladies would jump to retrieve my handkerchief should I toss it. Jane has none of their advantages. I can save her

from a life of hardship, of toil. Why should she refuse?''

"I don't know, I'm sure," Fitz mumbled.

Edmund walked home on air.

"My lady's back," Alfred greeted him.

Edmund returned to earth with a crash.

MISS GRACECHURCH sat by the open window in Jane's
sitting-room, reading. At least, a book lay open on her
lap. After perusing the same paragraph three times, she
had no notion what it was about. Nor was she aware of
the flowers in the garden, where her gaze was fixed,
though the peonies and tulips were at their best and the
fragrance of lilies-of-the-valley filled the air.

Half an hour ago, Lady Hornby had sent for Jane to
her boudoir. Interviews with her mother always upset
Jane, and this morning she was already in low spirits.

Yesterday, after hearing Lord Wintringham's sad
story, Jane had continued listless and unhappy. She was
deeply in love with the earl, yet she refused to trust him
with her true identity. Miss Gracechurch's heart bled for
her. She berated herself for having permitted the original masquerade, for letting it continue, for allowing secret meetings. If only she had realized sooner that what
started as a game had become a serious emotional en-
tanglement.

Her own yearning for Mr. Selwyn's...sympathetic
friendship had blinded her to Jane's needs at a critical
time. Not only had she neglected her duty, she had failed
the person she loved best in the world, who had no one
else to rely on.

The door opened and Jane trudged in. The spring was
gone from her step and her face was woebegone, though
she tried to smile at Gracie.

"The marchioness discovered last night that I rejected Lord Ryburgh and Lord Charles."

"Was she very angry?"

Jane nodded. Miss Gracechurch went to her, put an arm around her shoulders, and led her to the *chaise longue*. Sitting down beside her, she took her hands. "What did she say?"

"I had to tell her that I have no liking for any of my suitors. She is going to try this afternoon to persuade those two that they must not take my refusal seriously. I am to go to Almack's tonight and charm them so that they will offer again. But if they do, I shall refuse them again, Gracie!"

"I would not have you tied to a man you do not care for."

"I know I can count on your support. The marchioness says that if I am not wed by the end of the Season, I cannot expect another. I am too old, if you please, as though that were not her fault! But it will not be so bad to retire to Hornby, will it? We were always happy there. You shall be my companion instead of my chaperon, but we shall still study together, and sketch, and make music, and walk, and...deliver babies." Her voice dropped on the last words and she fell silent.

Gracie knew Jane's thoughts had flown to the last baby they had delivered together. She ventured one last plea. "Can you not bring yourself to tell Lord Wintringham..."

"No! I had rather mysteriously disappear, leaving both of us with happy memories, than sink myself in his opinion and have nothing to remember but his scorn." Her momentary animation faded. "I am so tired, Gracie. I slept badly last night. If I must go to Almack's tonight, I had best go and lie down for a while now."

She trailed out, each slow, weary step piercing Miss Gracechurch's conscience with a dart of self-reproach.

Self-reproach was futile. She could not sit still and watch Jane dwindling into an unfulfilled old maid. Half acknowledged was her own reluctance to return to the isolation of Hornby Castle, which had swallowed up her youth. There had been happy times—she had delighted in seeing her pupil grow up to be a cheerful, friendly, loving young woman—but circumstances had changed. Neither she nor Jane would find contentment at Hornby now.

She needed advice, and Mr. Selwyn was the obvious person to consult. Sending Thomas for a hackney, Miss Gracechurch hurried to her room to don pelisse, bonnet and gloves.

As the hackney rattled towards the City, she hoped she was right to expect the lawyer to be in his chambers at Lincoln's Inn at this hour. She could have sent a note. However, much as she wanted his counsel, still more she wanted the comfort of his presence. Even a sober governess of six-and-thirty needed . . . reassurance at times, she told herself.

She had walked with Mr. Selwyn in Lincoln's Inn Gardens once, and he had pointed out his chambers, so she knew where to direct the jarvey. Asking him to wait, she checked the names on the brass plate by the door and mounted the narrow stair. In the cramped outer office, the four clerks perched on high stools at their desks all turned to stare when she tentatively entered.

The eldest, a balding, gloomy-faced individual with ink-stained cuffs, stepped down and bowed. "Can I help you, ma'am?"

"My name is Gracechurch. I have no appointment but I hoped that Mr. Selwyn might spare me a few minutes.'' Feeling a blush steal up her cheeks, she wished she had not come to disturb him at work.

The clerk went away, and came back a moment later followed by Mr. Selwyn, a smile of welcome on his long, kind face.

''My dear Miss Gracechurch, this is a pleasant surprise. At least, I trust it is not an emergency?''

''Oh no, I . . . That is . . .''

''Come through to my office, where we can speak privately.'' He led the way to a small room bursting with books and papers, seated her, and closed the door. ''There, now we can be comfortable. If we were at home I should feel obliged to call my housekeeper as chaperon, but what can be more respectable than a lawyer's office?'' Sitting on a corner of his desk, he looked down at her gravely. ''Now, my dear, tell me what is the matter.''

Soothed by his calm attentiveness, she poured out the story, much of which he knew or had guessed. ''What really distresses me,'' she ended, ''is that Jane has given up. She is a courageous girl, who has never hesitated before to fight for what she wants—witness our setting out for London in an ancient and decrepit vehicle! Yet now, when her future happiness is at stake, she is sunk in apathy.''

''I wonder whether a shock might jolt her into action,'' mused Mr. Selwyn.

''A shock?''

''You say she is resigned to retiring to Hornby—with you. Suppose she had not that alternative. Suppose . . .'' He leaned forward, clasped her hands, and went on simply, ''My dear Miss Gracechurch, will you marry me?''

Taken utterly by surprise, she gazed up into his eyes. Sympathetic friendship—fustian! Reassurance—

fustian! What she wanted from this man was all the tenderness and ardour she saw there. Sober governess—fustian! She was a woman and she loved him. "Yes," she said.

So the sober lawyer pulled the sober governess into his arms and kissed her with all the thoroughness of a profession noted for its passion for thoroughness.

"David?" she murmured when she recovered her breath. Her head rested on his shoulder where, since her bonnet had fallen off, it fitted neatly against the angle of his jaw. "May I call you David?"

"If I may call you Claudia, my love."

"Of course, though I cannot promise always to answer to it at first. I am so used to Jane calling me Gracie. David, I cannot abandon her."

"I would never ask it of you. My hope is that when you tell her you are going to be my wife—" here he broke off for a quick kiss by way of punctuation "—it will precipitate a crisis which will work to everyone's advantage."

"Do you think so?" she said dubiously. "I cannot see how."

"If not, we shall try something else. There is always more than one way to settle a suit."

"How fortunate that I am to marry a lawyer! Very well, I shall tell her, David, but I dread the consequences."

UNACCUSTOMED TO SLEEPING in the afternoon, Jane awoke to a feeling of lassitude. She lay gazing up at the plaster mouldings on the ceiling, laurel wreaths and Tudor roses and the hunting-horn emblem of the Hornby coat of arms.

Hornby—how glad she had been to leave. How glad she would be to return, to sink back into a peaceful country life with dearest Gracie and Ella, and forget her disastrous foray to London. Tonight she would go to Almack's, to avoid another confrontation with her mother. She would save her courage for the moment when the marchioness learned she had no intention of marrying. Once, she had thought her courage equal to anything, but the realization that she loved Edmund and had damned herself in his eyes seemed to have drained every drop from her veins.

She blinked hard against the prickle of tears.

"You awake, my lady?" Ella peeked around the door, then came in carefully, bearing a tray. "I thought you'd fancy a cup o' tea."

"Thank you, that does sound good."

"There, now, let me plump up them pillows and you just sit here cosy and drink it up while I put out your things for tonight. What'll you wear?"

"I don't know, Ella. Whatever you think."

"Hows about your first ever ball gown? You've not worn it in a while, my lady, and never to Almack's as I recall. It's blue, to be sure, but his lordship don't go to Almack's."

"The blue satin and white net? That will do." It was a particularly pretty dress, with blue embroidered flowers and Valenciennes lace trimming. Perhaps looking her best would make her feel better. The tea was refreshing. She breathed in the fragrance of lilies-of-the-valley, wafting through the open window, and decided to carry a nosegay.

As Ella disappeared into the dressing room, Miss Gracechurch tapped on the door and came in. "Have you slept, Jane dear? You have a little more colour."

"I am much recovered. I shall get up in a few minutes. Come and have some tea, Gracie. Ella brought an extra cup."

Miss Gracechurch poured herself tea and perched on the end of the bed, delicate Limoges cup in hand. Puzzled, Jane saw that she was agitated, vacillating between intense, almost incredulous joy and anxious apprehension.

Carefully casual, Miss Gracechurch said, "Lord and Lady Hornby dine from home tonight, do they not?"

"Yes. You and I shall eat in comfort in my sitting room before we go to Almack's."

"Almack's! I had forgot. My wits have gone a-begging, I vow."

"And what has dispossessed them of their usual abode?" Jane asked, smiling.

"I... Oh dear, I hardly know...." Her cheeks pink, she set down her empty cup on the bed and took a deep breath. "My dear, wish me happy. Mr. Selwyn has asked me to be his wife."

"Has asked you to...? To marry him? And you have accepted?" For a moment Jane stared blindly into an empty future. She was cold, so cold; her head swam and a dreadful tightness constricted her chest. Then pride, good breeding, and her love for her dearest friend came to her rescue. Shaking herself, she said in a voice she scarce recognized as her own, "Forgive me, you took me by surprise. My darling Gracie, of course I wish you happy, though I have no doubt that you will be. Mr. Selwyn is the most amiable gentleman in the world."

Miss Gracechurch hugged her, and she found a temporary solace in the embrace that had soothed her childhood hurts and sorrows. But present reality intruded, in the form of Ella, asking had she finished her tea and was she ready to dress.

She slipped out of bed, her composure fragile as a blown glass goblet. In a dream, a bad dream, a nightmare, she washed and put on petticoat, satin slip, net frock, satin dancing slippers. She sat down at the dressing-table, her white face a stranger in the looking glass. Pearl ear-drops, pearl necklace.

"A touch o' rouge, my lady? Miss Pickerell'll lend me her ladyship's."

Dumbly, she shook her head and Ella began to arrange her hair.

Someone knocked at the door. Thomas, with a note for his sister.

"Beg pardon, my lady, but the lad said 'tis urgent."

Jane nodded, uninterested. Ella took the twist of paper, firmly shut her brother out, and opened it. She gasped.

"My lady, 'tis from Alfie... Mr. Alfred. He just found out Lady Wintringham's making his lordship go to Almack's tonight! Lor, he told us just in time. Now don't you worry, we'll think up summat to tell your ma why you didn't go. You've been a touch peaky all day."

"But I shall go, Ella." Watching, listening from some distant place, Jane wondered at her own icy calm. "I cannot put it off for ever. The worst will soon be over and then... and then.... Please put out my fur-lined cloak."

She was cold, so cold.

CHAPTER NINETEEN

ALMACK'S: the Marriage Mart; to the uninitiated, a set of less than magnificent assembly rooms in King Street, St. James's; to the eligible damsels of the ton, the holy of holies where only those judged worthy by the lady patronesses were admitted to the Wednesday subscription balls.

Eligible gentlemen had less difficulty gaining entrée. Without prospective husbands to be hunted, the purpose of the assemblies would vanish and with it the influence of the patronesses, the overweening doyennes of Society. A gentleman had only to remember to wear knee breeches rather than pantaloons, and to arrive before the doors closed at eleven o'clock, to be welcomed.

Correctly attired and on time, Edmund was unsurprised to be greeted with complaisance even by so high a stickler as Mrs. Drummond Burrell. Lady Jersey, with her usual hint of malice, twitted him on not having previously graced Almack's with his presence. His aloof dignity, and his status as a superior match, saved him from further reproach.

He moved on into the ballroom. Neil Gow's Band was fiddling away up on the balcony, and waltzing couples swirled about the floor. However ghastly this evening, Edmund reminded himself, tomorrow he would propose to Jane and the next day whisk her away to Dorset.

Glancing around, he saw Fitz nearby, talking to Lord Orme. Edmund was slightly acquainted with the viscount, a noted Town Beau, and did not care for him. Deciding to seek out Fitz later, he was about to go in search of a partner when Fitz saw him.

Lord Fitzgerald's thin face turned an unlikely shade of puce. He bounded forward and grabbed Edmund's arm.

"I say, Ned, you never come to Almack's."

"There is a first time for everything."

"But you told me you mean to offer... And besides, you won't like it above half, I assure you. Devilish flat company, low stakes, and the supper's a disgrace. You'd best just turn around and go home."

"Unfortunately, home is where Lady Wintringham arrived last night. My aunt considers it remiss of me to have avoided Almack's."

"Oh, lord!" Fitz blenched, then rallied. "Damme if she knows what it's like."

"I don't believe the countess has stepped within these sacred portals since she married off the last of your cousins, Wintringham," Lord Orme confirmed.

"You see, Ned? All you have to do is toddle off home and tell her you don't care for the place."

"So I shall, when I can tell her I have stood up with two or three suitable partners. I suppose Miss Chatterton is here? At least she has no designs upon me."

Over his shorter friend's head, Edmund glanced about the room. The waltz was over and the dancers were returning to the seats around the walls. Opposite the door where he stood, he caught a glimpse, between attentive gentlemen, of a young lady who reminded him of Jane.

When Jane was his wife, she should come to Almack's if she chose, he vowed. She should dress in silks and laces, bedeck herself in sapphires to match her eyes, and dance the night away.

Lord Orme had followed his gaze. "Admiring the latest heiress, eh?" he asked.

"Heiress?" said Edmund without interest.

"She's the only daughter. There's a brother, but Hornby has plenty for both by all accounts, and she's a pretty chit, into the bargain. Oh, haven't you met her? I'll present you to her if you like. That's Lady Jane Brooke."

At that moment, the girl looked across the room. Even at that distance, her eyes met Edmund's with a shock of recognition.

He shook off Fitz's hand, turned on his heel, and stalked out into the night.

Lady Jane Brooke, daughter of the Marquis of Hornby! His thoughts whirled. Pretending to be a nobody, she had made a May game of him, enticed him into abandoning formality, laughed at him behind his back like her fellow debutantes. She had undermined his walls and left him defenceless.

And somehow she had persuaded Fitz to betray him. Fitz knew everything, that was obvious. She had stolen from him a friend he could ill spare, flung him back to the agonizing isolation of his first days, weeks, months at Wintringham Abbey, surrounded by his girl-cousins' contemptuous derision.

How could a mask of enchanting friendliness hide such wanton cruelty? The girl he had fallen in love with did not exist.

Unseeing, unknowing, he found that his rapid stride had carried him to the river, to the Whitehall Stairs. Here he had embarked with Jane—with *Lady* Jane—for that delightful day at Richmond. That was the day he had first suspected that she might be illegitimate. How wrong he had been, a pathetic fool from first to last!

He stood, brooding. Below the embankment, the dark Thames slid past, glinting here and there with reflected light. Many a troubled soul had sought oblivion in those black waters, but that craven escape was not open to him. He was the Earl of Wintringham. Pride in his family and his rank was all that was left to him. He swung away from temptation and retraced his steps up Whitehall.

At Charing Cross he took the righthand fork, then turned up St. Martin's Lane. In the mean streets, alleys, and yards around Covent Garden, a mass of humanity swarmed in abject misery. Among them, surely, he ought to be able to count his own blessings. But, lost in a different sort of misery, he scarcely noticed the ragged waifs, the crippled beggars, the painted, half-naked, gin-reeking whores, who whined as he approached and jeered as he passed.

He walked until the short May night ended in a misty dawn. It was still too early for the City's clerks and shop-girls to be about, but a watchman on his rounds stared at the tall, bareheaded, forbidding gentleman in evening dress.

Returning homewards, Edmund trudged past St. Paul's—*Jane! Today we were to visit the bookshops of Paternoster Row. Today I was going to ask you to be my wife. Today, would you have ended the farce? Would you have mocked me to my face?* Alone, he made his way through the noisy bustle of Covent Garden Market, through the quiet, empty streets of Mayfair, and let himself into Wintringham House.

She had left him at Lady Wintringham's mercy. The special licence, his defiant symbol of freedom, lay useless in a drawer in his dressing-room.

The servants were still abed. Edmund sought his own, tossed and turned for a couple of hours, then rang for Alfred.

"Good morning, my lord." The valet marched across to the window, flung back the curtains to admit a flood of inappropriate sunshine, and said in a voice quivering with reproach, "My lord, Lady Jane cried herself to sleep."

"What flummery is this!" cried Edmund.

Alfred turned round. "It's no more than the truth, my lord. Upset already, she was, and then you ups and takes to your heels without so much as a how-de-do. It'll be a nine days' wonder, mark my words, Lady Jane Brooke rushing out of Almack's in a fit of weeping."

"So you are part of this conspiracy?" he asked bitterly. "My own servant laughing at my credulity! It is too late, Alfred. I am past believing any more lies."

"I wouldn't lie to you, my lord, honest, nor laugh at you. Haven't I been with you near twenty-five years and stuck by you through thick and thin? Only, Ellie—Miss Ella, that's Lady Jane's abigail—she wouldn't never have walked out with me, let alone told me nowt, if I hadn't've promised I'd keep mum. It weren't my secret, my lord, nor yet Ellie's, and she's as fond of her mistress as I . . . as I am of you, my lord, begging your pardon."

The passionate speech, the need to believe in the one person who had never let him down, convinced Edmund that Alfred spoke the truth as he knew it. Whether he had the truth from Ella was another matter. Jane running from Almack's in tears? Crying herself to sleep? His heart turned over at the thought.

Fitz would know, but he could not trust Fitz. Who was left to him? Selwyn must be aware of Lady Jane's deception, yet it was impossible to imagine the sober lawyer willingly lending himself to a cold-hearted trick. He, if anyone, might help Edmund separate lies from reality.

"Have my curricle brought round."

"But my lord, it's only just past six!"

"At once."

When he reached the house in Hart Street, the flustered maidservant showed him into the library.

"The master's not down yet, my lord," she said, wringing her hands.

"I shall wait."

He paced for a few minutes, oblivious for once of the books surrounding him, until Mr. Selwyn arrived, swathed in a red and green tartan dressing gown. After one glance at his visitor's face, the lawyer said over his shoulder, "Coffee." Shutting the door, he took Edmund by the elbow, made him sit down, and poured him a glass of brandy.

"I shall not appreciate this as it should be appreciated," Edmund said, attempting to smile.

"It will warm you. What has made you look as if you have seen a ghost?"

The syllables emerged with difficulty. "Lady Jane Brooke."

"Ah." Selwyn appeared to be oddly pleased with himself. "You had no suspicion? I had my doubts, even before we reached Wintringham Abbey, and when I voiced them I was enlightened by Miss Gracechurch, Lady Jane's governess and companion—and soon to be my wife."

"Your wife!" Edmund was jerked out of his absorption in his own troubles. "Yesterday I should have congratulated you most sincerely."

"You need not scruple to do so now. I count myself extremely fortunate to have won the affection of an admirable woman."

"Then I... Wait! You doubted Jane's story *before* you reached the Abbey? She was already playing a part?"

"I understand that her carriage broke down, and being forced to continue on the Mail she thought it best, with Claudia... Miss Gracechurch's concurrence, to travel incognito. Would you have believed a shabby young woman, arriving by Mail, to be the daughter of a marquis?"

"No," he admitted, then frowned. "But why did she not tell me when we met here? It was then no more than a joke."

"A joke?" Selwyn regarded him shrewdly. "I cannot feel that it is my place to explain Lady Jane's motives. Put it down to a lawyer's discretion, if you wish. Ah, here is our coffee. And toast, excellent, thank you." He poured them each a cup and passed the plate of buttered toast. "You will feel the better for a bite to eat. And then, my suggestion is that you go to St. James's Place and request an interview with Miss Gracechurch."

His mouth full of toast, Edmund stared, shrugged, and nodded. Brandy, food, and coffee in their turn made him feel slightly more human; however, they helped his uncertainty not at all. He did not know what to think so, as he drove to St. James's, he endeavoured not to think at all.

"Miss Gracechurch!" The butler's jaw dropped. He reread Edmund's card, consulted the long-case clock, glared at the footman who had summoned him from his breakfast, and, his face restored to proper woodenness, enquired aloofly, "*Now,* my lord?"

"Miss Gracechurch, now." Despite Edmund's haughty demeanour, despite the doubts that tormented him, the man's perplexity almost amused him. Jane's influence, no doubt. How could he live without her?

The Chinese salon he was shown into reminded him painfully of her liking for his Chinese chess set. The extravagance of red silk hangings and false bamboo reminded him that the daughter of the Marquis of Hornby must have countless eligible suitors who paid court to her in this room. Even if she did not despise him, the wealthy, captivating Lady Jane had no reason to choose an unsociable fool like himself.

He crossed to the window and looked out. The flower-filled garden reminded him of their first meeting in Hart Street. Nowhere could he escape her.

He turned as the door opened and Miss Gracechurch came in, her cap awry. The honey colour of her dishevelled curls reminded him of Jane's sleek tresses, and of his absurd apprehensions that they might be mother and daughter.

"I understand I am to wish you happy," he said harshly.

"Thank you, my lord. Will you be seated?"

Though she sounded calm, her hands were tightly clasped before her, white-knuckled. For the first time he recognized the difficulty of her position, as little better than a servant trying to curb the starts of a minx like Jane. He held one of the bamboo and ivory-brocade chairs for her and sat down opposite.

A minx like Jane—was that the whole story? Mischief gone awry, not cruel mockery? His anguish burst forth. "Why?" Unable to sit still, he strode back to the window, then flung round. "Why did she not tell me? At least when we met at Selwyn's. We could have laughed together about her masquerade at the Abbey."

"Would you have laughed, sir?"

The quiet question arrested him. Again he cast his mind back to that meeting. Stiff, frowning—she had teased him about the frown—he had apologized for kissing her. If she had revealed then that she was *Lady* Jane, would he have thought it a joke? "Probably not," he conceded. "But she had a hundred opportunities to explain later, after... after we became friends."

"She did not dare." In her agitation, Miss Grace-church joined him and laid her hand on his arm, looking up earnestly into his face. "Once you were friends, she was terrified of losing you."

He shook off her hand. "She has dozens of friends."

"She has dozens of acquaintances, my lord. You cannot imagine how lonely her life has been. She was her mother's pet until her brother was born. At the age of four—four!—she was exiled to the wilds of Lancashire, with none but servants for company. I went to her a year later, thank God, and then the marchioness tired of the boy, too, and sent him to us, until he was of age to go to school. Her father she saw at most once a year, her mother less often."

Edmund turned away to hide his heartache. Four! All too clearly he remembered his own agony at eleven years old.

Miss Gracechurch took his silence for disdain. "Can you not understand that having come to... to be fond of you, she could not bear to risk your turning from her in disgust?"

"Disgust?" he exclaimed, startled.

"Did you not tell her once that you abhorred deceit?"

"Did I? Perhaps I did. You mean she feared my contempt as much as I feared hers?"

It was her turn to be startled, but as she sought for words, the door opened. The pale, wan face with reddened eyes that appeared around it was the most beautiful sight Edmund had ever seen.

FIVE MINUTES EARLIER, that same sight, viewed in the mirror, had made Jane wince. "What a fright I look, Ella."

"His lordship won't care a groat, my lady, whether Miss Gracechurch has talked him round or no."

"I cannot go down!" she cried, panicking. "I shall wait until Gracie sends for me."

"Madam said get dressed and go down, my lady, and that's what you'll do. You're in no fit state to think for yourself, that's for sure. Now keep still, do, while I pin up your hair. There you go, you don't want nowt fancy this morning."

Starting down the stairs, Jane felt sick with apprehension. By the time she reached the first landing, she was certain her gay, periwinkle-blue muslin sprigged with white was quite the most inappropriate gown to wear on such a dreadful occasion. Mourning black would be more to the point. She half turned, ready to run back to the shelter of her chamber, but Ella stood there urging her on.

By the time she reached the bottom of the stairs, she had forgotten what she was wearing, forgotten her red-rimmed eyes. She stood shivering outside the door of the salon. Was he still there? What would he say? Would he look at her again with that bewildered hurt, quickly changing to cold fury, she had read across the width of Almack's ballroom?

Squaring her shoulders, she pushed open the door.

And suddenly there was nothing to fear. His heart in his eyes, Edmund took two hesitant steps towards her and she flew into the safe haven of his arms.

For a long moment they simply held each other tight, her face pressed to his shoulder, his cheek resting against her hair. Then she pushed away a little, looked up at him, and asked, "Are you very angry?"

"I thought you were laughing at me, Jane."

"I was, I do, you know I do, quite often, but only when you are odiously stiff and starchy," she said hopefully. "And even when you are My Lord Winter, I love you anyway."

His rueful smile reassured her. "I daresay I shall get used to you laughing at me, and even when you do, I love you anyway. I was going to ask you to marry me...."

"You *were*!" She stiffened in outrage, but he merely pulled her closer again.

"...and being an arrogant fool, I was quite certain you would have me."

"You really were going to ask plain Miss Jane Brooke to be your bride, your countess?"

"I went so far as to get a special licence. Then I discovered that your father is a marquis and I have scores of rivals."

"Does that mean you will not ask me, now, in case I refuse?"

"I hate to waste the special licence," he quizzed her.

"Hmmm. My mother would be pleased, I daresay, if we were to be married quickly and quietly and unobtrusively by special license."

"On the other hand, the banns read at St. George's, Hanover Square, and a vast, elaborate, Society wedding would best please my aunt."

"So the only question is, which of the two do we most wish to disoblige?"

He grinned, but said, "On the contrary, my dearest love, the only question is, how soon will you be my wife? Without you to laugh at me, I shall get stiffer and starchier until I cannot bend at the joints."

"A telling argument, Edmund, and you are right, we must not waste the special licence. By all means, let us be married at once!"

HARLEQUIN ROMANCE®

**Harlequin Romance
has love in
store for you!**

Don't miss next
month's title in

THE BRIDAL COLLECTION

A WHOLESALE ARRANGEMENT
by Day Leclaire

THE BRIDE *needed* the Groom.
THE GROOM *wanted* the Bride.
BUT THE WEDDING was *more* than
a convenient solution!

Available this month in
The Bridal Collection
Only Make-Believe
by Bethany Campbell
Harlequin Romance #3230

Available wherever Harlequin books are sold.

WED-8

HARLEQUIN HISTORICAL

CHRISTMAS

STORIES • 1992 •

Capture the magic and romance of Christmas in the 1800s
with HARLEQUIN HISTORICAL CHRISTMAS STORIES
1992—a collection of three stories by celebrated
historical authors. The perfect Christmas gift!

Don't miss these heartwarming stories, available in
November wherever Harlequin books are sold:

**MISS MONTRACHET REQUESTS by Maura Seger
CHRISTMAS BOUNTY by Erin Yorke
A PROMISE KEPT by Bronwyn Williams**

Plus, this Christmas you can also receive a FREE
keepsake Christmas ornament. Watch for details in all
November and December Harlequin books.

**DISCOVER THE ROMANCE AND MAGIC OF THE
HOLIDAY SEASON WITH HARLEQUIN HISTORICAL
CHRISTMAS STORIES!**